MW00927748

Her *Lucky* Charm

A Second Chance Romance

AMELIA KINGSTON

Her Lucky Charm
Copyright © 2018 Amelia Kingston
Second Edition

All rights reserved. No part of this publication may be
reproduced, distributed, or transmitted in any form or by any
means, including photocopying, recording, or other electronic or
mechanical methods, without the prior written consent of the
publisher, except in the case of brief quotations embodied in
critical reviews and certain other non-commercial uses permitted
by copyright law.

This novel is a work of fiction. Resemblance to actual persons,
things, living or dead, locales or events is entirely coincidental.

ISBN-13 (print): 978-1977016454

CONTENTS

CHAPTER ONE

Thursdays

Connor never liked Thursdays. Most people hate Mondays, the first day back to work. Back to reality. Connor loved Mondays. They're always busy with some new project he'd need to tackle. He thrived on the element of surprise, finding out what had fallen apart or popped up over the weekend. Monday was the day with the most unknowns and he loved that.

Some people don't like Wednesdays. Hump day. The farthest point from either weekend and truly where the drudgery of the week took hold. Not for Connor. Wednesdays he hit his stride. He'd finished the Monday crisis and pushed through all the routine little things on Tuesday. Wednesday he spread his wings, reaching farther and getting more done than any other day.

Then came Thursdays. They held no new challenges, just the implicit threat that nothing new could be started because the weekend was right around the corner. Connor hated stopping. Anything worth doing was worth doing until it was done. Nothing annoyed him more than the half-finished project, the half-lived life.

When Connor worked something, he was an avalanche, building speed and force until he was unstoppable. Like any other force of nature, he hated being controlled and functioned best with complete freedom. That was rare in the world of international corporate consulting, a field Connor didn't know existed until about five years ago when he finally started looking for an adult job.

He had never been a planner and liked to take things as they came, making decisions, big or small, based on his intuition. He lettered in almost every sport in high school but took a scholarship to play baseball because it felt right. The decision seemed that simple. He majored in communications because he liked talking to people.

It wasn't until halfway through his senior year of college that he started to wonder what was next. His dedication ensured he was a starter all four years of college, but he wasn't going to the Major Leagues. And he had no idea what jobs came from a degree in communications. As it turns out, not many, which was how he ended up getting his MBA. Connor didn't plan out his choices, but once made he committed to them fiercely. When something felt right, it was all he could see. He never doubted and he never turned back. He completed his MBA with honors even though he had no idea what to do with it.

In addition to being determined, Connor was clever and charming, two traits that always seemed to get him through despite his lack of planning. They got his foot in the door at Republic Consulting International as an acquisitions consultant. His job essentially entailed making sure everyone played nice and stayed happy during major corporate mergers. There were hundreds of people who handled the logistics and financial details of the merger. Brilliant people with accounting spreadsheets and lots of graphs. Connor understood most of what they did, but he would rather be the root canal practice patient at a third-rate dental school than spend his hours staring at spreadsheets all day. Luckily, he had a much rarer skill set. He knew people. He knew how to talk to them and he knew how to figure out what they wanted. All but one, Samantha Cane. Her desires had always been a mystery to him. He hadn't heard from her in eleven years and wasn't likely to anytime soon. Or so he thought before Rebecca called him into her office. On a Thursday.

"Connor, come in please. Have a seat," Rebecca said with a friendly smile on her face. She recruited Connor out of business school five years ago. A guest lecture on global markets turned into a debate between two students over price gouging of food sourcing. The argument quickly escalated into accusations of racism and socialist ignorance with threats of "taking it outside" being shouted across the lecture hall. Seeing the professor had completely lost control, Connor stood and demanded the room's attention with his calm confidence. He eased the tension with a joke and diffused the situation by finding common ground.

Rebecca saw dollar signs looking at the smiling faces around that lecture hall. Since then she gave

Connor a wide range of difficult projects, but no matter how challenging the client or how antagonistic the merger, everyone always raved about Connor. Women in particular couldn't get enough of his six-foot muscled frame and steely grey eyes. Rebecca being ten years older, his boss, and happily married made her mostly immune to his dashing ways.

Today she was more worried about his sharp tongue than his cute dimples. She knew he hated being pulled off a project before completion. Plus, he was superstitious about starting projects on Thursdays. Usually she obliged him his idiosyncrasies because he got the job done better than any of her other consultants. Today she was going to make him break both of his rules.

"What's up? Did you want an update on the Stevens-Walker project? Everything is on track for the seventh—" Connor launched into his update as soon as he sat down.

"No need for that. I'm sure you're on top of it." Rebecca sat down behind her desk as she cut him off. "In fact, since the Stevens-Walker merger is basically complete, I'm going to have you hand it over." Like ripping off a band aid, she made the declaration fast and without hesitation. She clicked away at her computer, not making eye contact with Connor, continuing with work as if she hadn't just ruined his day.

"I would really rather wait until I've finished the project I'm working on." His tone reflected the scowl that permeated his usually jovial face. "You know I hate to leave anything unfinished." Connor was curt but professional.

"And usually I'd let you. But this is a major new

4

client. Phillips, Morrissey & Tanner is acquiring Keiretsu International Holdings to add an Asian branch to their corporate litigation department. They've hired us to facilitate the transition."

"And I'd love to help them with that, after the seventh when I've finished with the Stevens-Walker merger," Connor replied with a sly smile. The name Phillips, Morrissey & Tanner sounded familiar, but he didn't take the time to search his memories for why. He was too focused on the fight at hand. Rebecca turned to face him, interlacing her fingers on her desk and squaring her shoulders. She didn't return his smile.

"If I thought it could wait until the seventh, I would consider it. Obviously since I have already made the decision to re-assign you—" She paused for a moment to make it clear she had made up her mind. "I don't think it can. While everything points to a smooth transition since this is a mutually beneficial deal, those are usually the ones that go sideways. I'd take the devil I know any day. Right now, both parties are being amicable, but you are the best I have and I need you to make sure it stays that way." Rebecca was firm and even in her response.

"Who is the primary point of contact at each agency?" Connor asked with a sigh, tacitly accepting his reassignment. He knew any further push back would be wasted energy.

"I am waiting on the contact for Keiretsu, but I have the e-mail from PMT here. Samantha Cane. I'll send you her contact information. Please reach out to her immediately and get the introductions out of the way."

Connor froze. His mouth fell open and his heart

stopped. He might think about Samantha Cane almost every day and Google her with some regularity, but he hadn't heard her name in over a decade. He tried to remember to blink as he stared at Rebecca blankly.

"Connor? You okay?" Rebecca's voice rang in his ears and he knew he should say something, but his brain was too busy trying to process the last five minutes.

"I can't," were the only words he was able to muster.

"Excuse me? What do you mean you can't?" Rebecca was losing her patience.

"Rebecca, listen. I just can't take on a new project right now. I don't think you understand how much more is needed to close the Stevens-Walker deal." He was stumbling over his words, fumbling to find an excuse that didn't require him to explain his past with Samantha. Memories of her flooded his mind. He remembered the way she smirked, the sound of her voice, the smell of her hair, the way her lips tasted, how her naked body felt underneath his. He remembered every second of their nights together, including their last. A sharp pain hit him in the chest like a knife plunged deeply and then twisted. A wound that would never heal.

"I don't have time for this, Connor. Frankly, this is non-negotiable."

"Nothing is ever non-negotiable." Connor tried his usual charm, knowing on Rebecca it wouldn't go far.

"This is." Rebecca didn't budge.

"Rebecca, believe me when I tell you I'm not the guy for this job." A hint of desperation crept into

Connor's voice. It made Rebecca pause for just a moment.

"I'm not...This isn't..." Connor was at a loss for words. He refused to admit he had a personal issue with taking this project, with working with Samantha Cane, but he didn't have any other excuse. He looked like he was just being difficult.

"Connor, unless you can give me a damn good reason why you can't get this job done, this conversation is over." Rebecca waited on Connor's response, half curious, half irritated. He didn't make one. He just dropped his head down and started at the floor, letting out a painful sigh and sounding exhausted.

"Alright then. Hand over whatever is left of the Stevens-Walker merger to Jeff and get in touch with Ms. Cane." There was the knife again, twisting a little harder.

Connor skulked out of Rebecca's office like a moody teenager. There didn't seem to be any way around it. He was going see Samantha Cane again. Soon.

Fuck Thursdays.

CHAPTER TWO

The E-mail

Connor Grayson. His name seemed to pulse on her computer screen in time to the racing beats of her heart. It'd been thirty minutes since his e-mail popped into her inbox and all she managed to do was stare at it in petrified terror. What could he possibly have to say to her after all these years? Every inch of her yearned to know, but she was too scared to open his e-mail and find out. It was the first correspondence between them in eleven years.

There wasn't a word in the English language capable of describing what they were to each other, but they weren't friends. They never had been. Not in high school and certainly not now. How could they be after what she did? Her stomach churned with the memory of how she treated him. She knew he was lost to her forever. It wasn't how she wanted it, but how she needed it. He wasn't in her life and he never could be.

She sat behind a mahogany desk, staring blankly at the view from her 32nd floor corner office. Underneath her perfectly tailored suit, that familiar empty feeling surged in the hollow of her chest. She spent years trying to fill it with her ever increasing goals for professional and financial success. The emptiness was her constant companion. It drove her to work longer hours, make harder sacrifices, and do the jobs no one else wanted. It got her here, on the verge of being the youngest partner ever at one of the most prestigious law firms in the country, Phillips, Morrissey & Tanner.

At twenty-eight, Samantha Cane thought she had the perfect life. Amazing job. Great house. Awesome car. Phenomenal wardrobe. Box seats at the opera. On her thirty-year plan, she was well ahead of schedule. And the empty feeling was stronger than ever.

Connor's e-mail sat in her inbox, taunting her.

From: Connor.Grayson@RepublicConsulting.com
To: Samantha.Cane@PMTLaw.com
Subj: Introductions and Meeting Time

A thousand scenarios played out in her head. Maybe he forgave her and he wanted to talk. Maybe it was another Connor Grayson. It wasn't a common name, but surely there was at least one other Connor Grayson in the world. Maybe he finally got the nerve to tell her off. Worst of all the possibilities floating around in her imagination, he got married and wanted to introduce her to his new beautiful wife.

Over the years she typed up hundreds of messages

to him. Texts, emails, and even handwritten letters. She poured her heart out, begging for forgiveness, asking to see him. In the end she always deleted or burned them, destroying the evidence of her weakness.

Tears began to form in the corners of her eyes as the memory of her last words to him slithered up the back of her mind and into her conscious thoughts. It made her feel sick. She bit down on the inside of her cheek bringing a metallic taste and the distraction of pain to her rescue. She wouldn't cry. She hadn't cried since their last night together.

She willed herself to look anywhere but down at her computer screen. The papers on her desk. The awards framed on her wall. The city bustling outside her floor-to-ceiling windows. None of it could hold her attention. Her traitorous eyes remained glued to the bold type of the unread e-mail.

She tried to think of anything but Connor and the words he might want to say to her. Her mind refused to obey when she desperately tried not to think back to their nights together. Now over a decade old, the memories still made her skin tingle and her cheeks flush. He had never spoken more than a few words to her, but the last three were "I love you." When she was seventeen, she gave him her virginity and her heart.

A voice calling her name made Samantha start, bringing her back to the real world. The air was thick with her memories. Her thoughts still clouded by them.

"Ms. Cane, do you want me to confirm the appointment with Mr. Grayson for this week?" Tammy asked. Her assistant was a sweet, but moderately annoying chubby girl in her mid-twenties. Yet again Tammy came into Samantha's office without knocking despite being told repeatedly to do so. Samantha had to be explicit in her directions to Tammy and never expect too much. She wasn't as bright, educated, or experienced as a lot of the other applicants who had interviewed for the position. Samantha hired her because of her understated dedication and genuine desire to help people.

Tammy arrived for her interview fifteen minutes early on a day that was spectacularly busy for the firm. They landed a major case slated to start litigation in three days. It was an all-hands-on-deck effort for the firm. When Tammy walked up, the receptionist was almost in tears, overwhelmed with the influx of tasks the lawyers without assistants had been handing her. Tammy immediately asked what she could do and started taking on some of the smaller tasks. She made copies, got coffee, walked files from one office to the next for forty-five minutes.

Samantha was underwhelmed with Tammy's interview and had written her off. She was walking Tammy to the elevator, giving her the "we'll be in touch" speech, when the receptionist bounded over and hugged her.

"Thank you so much! You're a lifesaver," the receptionist said with genuine sincerity. Samantha looked confused and Tammy meekly replied she was happy to help before hopping in the elevator and leaving without any explanation.

"What was that about?" Samantha asked.

"Oh, I was so swamped. When she got here, she jumped in and started helping me with some of the requests for the other associates," the receptionist chirped.

Tammy hadn't said a word. She didn't do it because she thought it would land her the job. She just saw someone who needed a bit of help and did what she could. She hadn't even thought to mention it in the interview. Samantha didn't interview anyone else.

"Ms. Cane?" Tammy was still standing there, pen and paper in hand, waiting for her to answer.

"I'm sorry, Tammy. I didn't hear you knock." The comment wasn't lost on Tammy who looked down sheepishly. "What did you say?" Her mind was trying to shake off the fog and piece together what Tammy said. She asked about confirming a meeting. What meeting? Whose name did she say? Mr. Grayson? That couldn't be right.

"Are you okay? You look a bit..." Thankfully Tammy didn't finish her thought. Samantha didn't want to know what she looked like right now. Panicked would be her guess at the word Tammy knew better than to say.

"I'm fine. What did you need?" Samantha was more curt than usual, but Tammy was familiar with the clipped tone. Samantha used it with everyone, so she didn't take it personally.

"Did you want me to confirm the meeting this week with Mr. Grayson? You have an availability Wednesday afternoon."

She had said his name. Samantha wasn't dreaming. She couldn't form a response. She was staring at Tammy with a confused look on her face, something Tammy had never seen before.

"From Republic Consulting International. Did you not see his e-mail?"

Samantha gave Tammy access to her work e-mail in order to keep her schedule, update her contacts, and other general office management things. Samantha never mixed her personal life—what little there was of one any way—and her professional life, so it never concerned Tammy could read any e-mail she wanted. Immediately, Samantha's eyes shot down to her computer screen at the still bold e-mail sitting unopened in her inbox. Before she had time to second guess herself, she opened it and read in a half-whisper, trying to make sense of it while Tammy still stood in her doorway.

From: Connor.Grayson@RepublicConsulting.com
To: Samantha.Cane@PMTLaw.com
Cc: Jeremy.Slone@PTMLaw.com;
Rebecca.Smith@RepublicConsulting.com
Subj: Introductions and Meeting Time
Ms. Cane-
My firm's services have been retained to assist Phillips, Morrissey, & Tanner with the upcoming merger with Keiretsu International Holdings. I would like to schedule a time this week to do some preliminary introductions and discuss the way forward on this project.
Please let me know when you are available.
Looking forward to working with you and your team.
Sincerely,
Connor Grayson
Acquisitions Consultant

The last line of his signature was a small picture of him wearing a tailored navy suit and a familiar easy smile. Without a doubt this, was her Connor.

She read the e-mail three times, trying to

understand it. It was from Connor, but it wasn't. At least, not him personally. It was basically a form letter, the same introduction letter he sends to all his clients. He copied her boss and someone else from his firm. A woman.

Was she his partner? His boss? Something more?

Samantha's mind was lost in a world of what-ifs until the sound of Tammy tapping her pen on her notepad brought her back. Samantha swallowed hard, choking down all the possibilities and questions.

"Yes. Please schedule the meeting. Have all the staff who will be working on the Keiretsu merger available and reserve a conference room." Samantha's voice was flat as Tammy scribbled down her few simple directions before leaving.

Alone again in her office, Samantha read and re-read Connor's e-mail until the reality started to sink in. There were a few things she knew for sure.

She would be seeing Connor the day after tomorrow.

He either didn't remember her or didn't care.

Their time together hadn't meant to him what it meant to her.

She bit down on her cheek again, this time the metallic taste filling her entire mouth.

CHAPTER THREE

The Beginning

Eleven years ago...
The summer of Samantha's junior year she was selected for the state's prestigious debate team. As far as high school extracurricular activities go, it was the cream of the crop. After this summer, Samantha would be one step closer to Stanford. If she could get a letter of recommendation from the team's coach, a Stanford grad himself, she'd basically be a lock. This summer was crucial, an important step on her thirty-year plan.

High school valedictorian.

Stanford for undergrad.

Top ten law school.

Ace the bar.

Kick ass in a prestigious law firm.

Make partner.

Rule the world.

Live happily ever after.

The fact that at seventeen Samantha had a thirty-year plan should tell you everything you need to know about her. She was mature beyond her years to put it mildly. At nine she decided nicknames were for babies and insisted everyone call her Samantha. Anyone who called her anything else, teachers, classmates, even her friends, would be completely ignored. Her father was the only exception. She let him call her Sammie.

Her father had always been her favorite person in the world. As an only child, he was her first friend. Despite being exact opposites, they were two peas in a pod. He was easy, fun, and confident. She was challenging, stoic, and unsure. For as long as she could remember Samantha thought everything in her life was a test. She lived in absolutes. Her dad was the only person who could make her laugh when the self-doubt seemed like it would crush her.

There was only success or failure.

Samantha had lots of friends, but none were very close. She would smile and joke, pretend to be easygoing, but no one really knew her. She preferred it that way. She was too driven to want the distraction of real relationships. School was something she needed to get through, not an experience to enjoy.

She was the junior class president and had her eyes on the presidency for senior year. She had a 4.2 GPA thanks to several honors classes. SATs were in the bag. She had aced them last year. All signs pointed to Stanford, but for some reason that didn't seem to take any of the pressure off. Every day was an uphill sprint on uneven ground. One false step would send her tumbling back down. She had a few panic attacks last year during finals. It was never during any of the actual tests. She was fine once she had the pencil and paper in front of her. It was more like stage fright. The anticipation tortured her. She spent hours the night before a test listening to the voice in the back of her head.

You aren't good enough.

Everyone will find out you can't hack it.

This failure is going to ruin the rest of your life.

That voice was the same one running through her head as she stood outside the debate room, glued to her spot in the hallway, unable to move. She couldn't take a full breath. She got her first debate topic the week before. Is national security more important than personal privacy? She was ecstatic, diving right into her research with a singular dedication. She had examples, quotes, and case studies all memorized. She rehearsed her opening remarks in her bathroom mirror all morning. She knew she could do this. But then there was that voice. And it seemed to get louder the closer she stepped to the door.

You are going to forget everything as soon as you stand up!

You are going to look like a fool.

Logically she knew today was just a practice debate between teammates, a way for their coach to get to know their debate styles and evaluate their strengths. In her head, today was an interview for the life she wanted to have. It was the first of a string of dominoes that had to fall to keep her on her thirty-year plan. Panic rushed over her as her heart raced and her palms started sweating. She wanted to call her dad for a pep talk, but she was too ashamed. She hated herself for not being in control. She hated herself for being weak.

"Hey, are you alright?" a deep voice called from the end of the hallway. Startled, she was pulled out of her self-loathing as she turned to face the source of the words.

Connor Grayson. She knew who he was, even though they'd never actually met. They weren't friends. They weren't really anything.

He graduated this year and had a full ride to UCLA for one of the sports he played. Samantha couldn't remember which, but there was a sports camp on campus during summer.

They were only a grade apart, but they lived in different worlds. They never spoke to each other, not because they didn't like each other, but because they'd never had any reason to. Each was popular in their own way. Samantha was an academic, in lots of clubs, and knew lots of people. She took honors classes and was in student government. Connor was on every varsity sports team. He knew everyone in the school but had a close group of friends he spent most of his time with. They each existed happily in their individual worlds, which until now had never overlapped.

Samantha was frozen in place. Connor walked up to her slowly, like she was an injured animal he was afraid of spooking.

He was beautiful, even in his gym shorts and the sleeves cut off his T-shirt down to his rib cage. It was a look Samantha never liked. If you don't want your shirt to have sleeves, just buy a tank top! Judging by the sweat running down his chest, he just finished working out. Her eyes traced over his body from his tan and muscular legs to his hard abs. When he pulled up his shirt to wipe a bead of sweat off his cheek, she let her eyes linger on the exposed skin at his waist. The hint of a muscular V at his hips pointed down to the area Samantha wasn't brave enough to look at. Her eyes continued up to his thick arms and strong shoulders until they landed on his face. That was where she saw it.

Pity.

His beautiful face showed nothing but a deep worry. This boy who'd never said a word to her had nothing but pity for her. It confirmed everything the voice said. Every tiny insecurity came rushing back. She wasn't worthy of anything but pity and disdain.

Connor was now right in front of her. She could smell the salty sweat on his skin mixed with the cool musk of his body wash as he reached out to touch her arm. Despite his alluring scent and the growing warmth on her skin in anticipation of his touch, she was furious at him and the pity in his eyes.

This stranger had no right to judge her. He had no idea who she was or what she was capable of. She had to show him she was in control. Show herself she was strong. Prove she wasn't what the voice of self-doubt kept telling her she was.

She slapped away his outstretched arm. When her eyes met his there wasn't an ounce of panic left, just a passionate fury. The flush on her cheeks and the intensity in her eyes made her so strikingly beautiful Connor let out a short gasp. He was suddenly unable to catch his breath.

In the same heartbeat, Samantha grabbed his sweaty shirt, pulling him down onto her lips. She kissed him like she was a queen and he was her slave. She would dominate him, leaving no room for his pity or her doubt. She felt his arms wrap around her waist as his mouth opened, giving in to her. She slid in her tongue, owning every inch of him.

She broke away from his hold and looked up into his eyes again. They were silver pools filled with a reckless desire. It brought a wicked smile to her face. Lust had overtaken pity. A fist full of his shirt still in her hand, she pulled him into the bathroom behind her. She wasn't done with him yet.

Once inside, she reached behind him and locked the door. They were alone. She heard his heart racing, his breath heavy and hot on her neck as she stood on tiptoes to whisper into his ear.

"Make me come." It wasn't a plea. It was a command. Three dirty little words she'd never said aloud before, much less to a living, breathing man whose tensed body was pressing against her own. The words didn't even sound like her own. Her entire sexual experience was limited to a few make-out sessions with some fully clothed dry humping. She didn't know what she wanted him to do. She didn't have to. Connor was going to do as he was told.

Before Samantha had time to let the doubt creep back in, he wrapped her up in his arms and set her down on the edge of the counter. He stepped between her legs, spreading them gently, while pulling her arms up around his neck. One hand caressed her breast while the other slid up her skirt and tickled the inside of her thigh as his lips met hers with fervent devotion. Unable to control the excitement of being touched like this for the first time, Samantha let out a soft moan. She could feel him getting hard against her thigh and it gave her a kind of sexual power she'd never known before.

"Is this what you want?" he asked in a pleading whisper as he slipped his fingers inside her wet panties.

"Shhh. No talking," she reprimanded him. She loved the sound of his deep sensual voice, but she didn't want to ruin the moment with words. A spell had been cast to bring them here, to make her this woman. She wouldn't risk any words that may break it. She answered his question by tightening her grip on the nape of his neck and bringing his lips back to hers. She moaned against them as the heat started to build in waves across her body.

The excitement of her newfound sensuality and the bliss of his touch didn't take long to bring her over the edge. She came in his arms, her raspy breaths against his lips, melting into him. Any self-doubt died with the last strokes of his fingers. She asked him to make her come, but he did more than that. He made her feel powerful and deeply sexy.

She rested her forehead against his chest and let them stay connected for just a few breaths, what felt like only a heartbeat to Connor, before she pushed him away. In one motion she pulled down her skirt and jumped off the counter. She strutted to the door, paused for just a second, looking back at him over her shoulder.

"Thank you. I think you might be my new lucky charm," she said with a seductive smile.

And with that, Samantha Cane left Connor Grayson standing alone in the girl's bathroom with the biggest hard on of his life and a look of complete confusion on his face.

CHAPTER FOUR

The Aftermath

Eleven years ago...

Samantha's cheeks were still glowing when she breezed into the debate hall, without a care in the world. Being with Connor made her feel in control of her life for the first time. The release he gave her silenced that inner voice.

Unfortunately for her debate partner, it meant she was unbeatable. She destroyed him. She always had the knowledge necessary to win and Connor had given her the confidence to match it. She basked in the euphoria of her victory for the remainder of the day, barely listening to the other debates. Her mind was calm as she replayed the brutal defeat over and over in her head during the entire drive home, reveling in an overwhelming sense of pride and accomplishment.

It wasn't until she was back in her room, lying on

her bed that she let her mind wander to what she had done with Connor. She could convince herself it was a dream if the vividness of the memory didn't still bring warmth to her thighs and a blush to her cheeks. How could she have done that? Why did he let her? What must he think of her? Samantha desperately wanted to confide in someone. She only had three friends she talked to outside of school, and never about anything like this.

Brent was her closest guy friend. Even if she wasn't sure he had a crush on her, he would not be someone she could confess a sexy tryst to. Kimberly was too much like Samantha, inexperienced and shy. She wouldn't understand, must less provide any useful insight. Monica was the typically boy crazy friend. She had more boyfriends and more adventures than Samantha and Kimberly combined, although that wasn't saying much. Samantha debated calling Monica for two hours, going as far as dialing her number a couple times only to flinch at the thought of how to start. Samantha desperately wanted to know what someone else would think of the whole thing. All the thoughts and questions circling around in her head were going to drive her mad.

The more she thought about telling anyone, the more she knew no one except Connor could tell her what it meant. More than any sense of embarrassment or the worry that Monica wouldn't believe her, it was the unshakable feeling that she and Connor had shared something personal and private that kept her from calling. She imagined having to say out loud those words again she'd whispered in his ear. Describing the things they did together seemed like a betrayal. A terrifying thought gripped Samantha at that realization. Did he feel the same way? Was he going to tell anyone? Had he already? The rest of Samantha's restless night was spent wondering if she was going to be a joke to everyone she knew by morning after Connor told everyone they knew.

Connor's restless night was spent wondering when he'd get to see—or more importantly touch—Samantha Cane again. When she stormed out of that bathroom, leaving him with only a thank you and a smile, he was completely mystified. Even before that she had enchanted him. Every moment with her was intoxicating. He had to spend fifteen minutes in the bathroom after she left to recover his composure. Since then she was all he could think about. When he finally walked out of the bathroom, he went to the door she had been standing in front of. He watched her from the small window, making sure he wasn't seen. She was standing behind a podium making some sort of speech. She had the same unmistakable fury in her eyes and was commanding the entire room. She looked like a dynamic force. Connor couldn't help but smile at the sight of her. Standing there in front of that room, owning her space, she was the sexiest thing he'd ever seen.

Connor finally dragged himself away from the window after Samantha finished her speech and sat down to a round of applause. He was thirty-five minutes late for his summer camp, missing almost the entire team meeting. He lost all focus and couldn't seem to concentrate on much of anything.

After his restless night thinking of Samantha, he wasn't performing much better at practice. His coach was riding him all day. He was exhausted and frustrated. Sports always came easy and having a slump was something new to him. As much as he tried to deny it, he knew his frustration had to do with wanting to see Samantha again.

For an entire week, Connor walked past the debate hall at various times trying to catch a moment to talk to Samantha or at least to steal a knowing smile. But each time they were either busy or the room was empty. Each day he lingered longer and was later to practice. His coach was pissed now, not only because he was late but because he still hadn't come out of his slump. His coach kept calling him lazy and unfocused.

Distraction was a new problem for Connor. He was known for being singularly focused. He did only one thing at a time and he did it with everything he had. It was his secret to lettering in three sports. Each one of his coaches knew that he wouldn't start practicing for the next sport's season until the current sport was finished. At first, they thought it meant he wouldn't be as conditioned as the rest of the team, but each year he would show up with a fierce dedication which overcompensated for the lack of field time. Now something changed. Samantha kept him from attaining that same singular focus. He needed to fix that fast.

The Friday before their first scrimmage game Connor's coach gave him an ultimatum to show up and play or he'd call the UCLA coach to ensure Connor rode the bench his first year. Connor didn't necessarily believe he could or would be benched, but it was all the motivation he needed to find Samantha. Instead of warming up with the team, he waited outside of the debate room for twenty minutes, pretending to be texting on his phone. He wanted to catch her alone, but if he couldn't, he'd take her any way he could get her. The room was clearing out. He refused to look up from his phone, but every one of his senses was on high alert for any sign of her, her voice, her smell, the shape of her entering the hallway.

After everyone else had cleared out he peeked inside the room and saw she was finishing up a conversation with her teacher. She picked up her bag and was headed towards him. Before she looked up and saw him, he turned away, suddenly terrified to face her. When he heard the door to the debate hall open, he froze with his back still to her, holding his breath. She took two steps toward him and then stopped. Was she going to come up to him? Did she even recognize him? Connor's breath caught in his throat. They stood in the hallway, neither moving, both feeling the electric current surging between their bodies, charging the air around them, ready to shock them both. She was the first to move. It was a slow pivot on the balls of her feet towards the exit. She was leaving. He wasn't going to let her, his desire suddenly restoring his resolve.

Connor spun around and grabbed her wrist. Samantha's eyes went to the hand that softly, but intensely held her back. A second ago, staring at his broad shoulders and athletic back, she was sure he was intentionally ignoring her and wanted nothing more than to escape from him down the hallway as fast as possible. Now, as she raised her eyes and met that oddly familiar gaze, she wanted to melt back into his chest like the last time his hands were on her. He saw it on her face, already able to read her body like a book. A sly smile crept onto his full lips as he pulled her into him.

"My turn," was all he whispered before their lips

connected. It felt like coming home. It was passionate, but more than that it was familiar, warm, and welcoming. It was a soft balm on the raw nerves she had all week from thinking of him, missing him. How could a place she had only been once feel like where she was meant to be? She put her arms around his neck and he pulled her against him as he walked them both back into the women's bathroom. He lifted her up and pinned her against the wall as her legs wrapped around his waist. Just like their last rendezvous, one of his hands caressed her breast while the other moved up her thigh. His need for her was consuming. She pushed his hand off her thigh sternly with one hand as the other pressed into his chest. He pulled back and let her down to the ground, her rejection making him unsure of himself. Samantha had never been surer of anything. She stepped around him and locked the bathroom door before turning back to him with that seductive smile.

"Your turn," she said as she pushed him up against the wall.

She kissed him with a gentle keenness as she unbuckled his pants. He was already completely hard as she sank to her knees in front of him. She had never seen an erection before, much less put one in her mouth. She had no idea what she was doing. In any other part of her life, she couldn't do anything the first time without being paralyzed with immense fear, regardless of how much preparation she had done. With Connor, she didn't panic. She didn't doubt herself. She didn't even think. She just followed her body in response to his.

Within minutes of putting him in her mouth he was coming, his hands in her hair, and her name on his lips. The way she took control, the way she knew exactly what he wanted before he knew to ask for it, was irresistible. It felt like losing control and taking it back at the same time. Before he was ready, she stood up, and walked back to the door with a sexy strut that was all her own.

"You're welcome, lucky charm," she cooed back at him with a soft simper before stranding him alone in a bathroom again.

Connor closed his eyes, taking several deep breaths, and trying to commit the image of her face with that smile to his memory forever. After he collected himself, he jogged out to the field and played the best game of his life. He never knew, but Samantha watched him from behind the bleachers that night. She only meant to say for the first few minutes, but she was intoxicated by the effortlessness of every athletic move his body made. His easy confidence on that field was the sexiest thing she had ever seen.

CHAPTER FIVE

Introductions

In his final act of petty defiance, Connor waited until
Monday to send an e-mail to Samantha. He told
himself it was just to spite Rebecca. In reality, it took
him the full three days to figure out what to say to
her, or in this case, what not to say. He thought about
what he wanted to tell Samantha Cane a million times
over the years. He pictured everything from
screaming at her until his voice gave out to dropping
to his knees and begging her to tell him why.

Why did she walk away?

That question has haunted him for almost half of
his life.

In the end, pretending she didn't exist was his only
option. Deny that once she had been his entire world,
his everything. That was going to be infinitely more
difficult when he came face to face with her.

He sent the e-mail to her first thing Monday

morning. He told himself he wasn't waiting for her response, that he was merely continuing with his normal Monday routine. It was a lie. He was glued to his computer, obsessively clicking refresh on his e-mail, waiting for her response. He even had his assistant confirm the internet server was still working, convinced he wasn't receiving any e-mails, despite having received several messages from people other than Samantha Cane.

He couldn't put his phone down the entire hour of the morning board meeting which he was paying absolutely no attention in. When he got back to his office, he kept frantically glancing at his e-mail inbox as he scrolled through the initial contract between his company and Samantha's law firm. Phillips, Morrissey & Tanner. He needed to get used to referring to the company by its name instead of its relationship to Samantha. That would be fun to explain to Rebecca if he slipped up. He spent the rest of the morning reminding himself to be a professional. The fact that Samantha was involved was just another complication. Every project had its special circumstances. He'd never had a challenge he wasn't able to overcome. That's why he was the top Acquisitions Consultant at Republic Consulting.

He checked his e-mail again. Still nothing.

With the start of every new project, Connor had Brianna, his assistant, put together dossiers on all the principal, both the companies and the associates who Connor would have to keep happy. These weren't anything too invasive, just a middle ground between a standard business biography and a full background check. It consisted mostly of what could be found from internet searches and social media. They included basic information such as, hometown, college attended and major, family situation, personal likes, and hobbies. With a little research, he could find an easy icebreaker for anyone. A little birdie told me you're a Buckeye's fan? Great season they're having this year!

Connor was a firm believer in first impressions. It may be manipulative, but the trick allowed him to form an instant, although tentative, bond. Connor learned early people are willing to do more for someone they like than someone they just work with. People care more about you when you seem to care about them.

Connor reviewed the dossiers, beginning with the principle at Keiretsu Holdings, Mr. Hirotami Kojima. He was on the younger side for a Japanese executive, only thirty-seven, which means he's likely driven and goal oriented. Connor's thoughts again wandered to Samantha. He knew she was also fiercely committed and focused. Connor made a note of the potential personality conflict, jotting down a few notes on how to get them off on the right foot. Hirotami was single. He attended a Japanese university, but got his MBA from Northwestern University, meaning he was fluent in English. He had been working for Keiretsu Holdings for the past eight years. His social media posts weren't family and friends. They were expensive looking meals, tiny plates on linen tablecloths in softly lit dining rooms. Hirotami was a serious foodie. Connor was looking forward to abusing the corporate expense account for some business dinners.

The next profile was on Jeremy Slone, Samantha's boss. Again Connor reminded himself not to think of everyone in relation to Samantha. It was a constant struggle. It unsettled him how quickly his world seemed to revolve around her again. Slone was a senior partner at Phillips, Morrissey & Tanner in his early sixties. Wife number three has been around for the past two years and worked as an interior designer. Connor noted she was about Samantha's age, and then chastised himself for it. Not everything was about Samantha! Slone was a well-established partner, past the point of needing to turn any heads. Slone's primary concern for the merger was going to be keeping the train on the tracks.

Samantha's file sat in front of Connor. He half-heartedly followed her life over the years. He knew she got into Stanford for her undergrad and stayed for law school. He knew she turned her internship at Phillips, Morrissey & Tanner into her current job, meaning they lived in the same city. He didn't know if she was married.

He checked his e-mail again. Still nothing.

Over the years he kept tabs on where she was and what she was doing, but he was always afraid to dig too deep. He told himself it was because he wasn't that curious. The truth was he would rather hope she was single than know she wasn't.

Wondering about her personal life was worse in the past few years. The first time he received a wedding invitation from one of his high school friends he immediately thought of Samantha. It was a reflex. His mind instantly pictured her in a white dress, smiling at some other guy. Connor had been in a bad mood for the rest of the day. It was the closest he ever came to reaching out to her. The desire to find out what her life was like almost overwhelming. And here it was, sitting in front of him, in her dossier.

He was petrified. He sat there for twenty minutes alternating between staring at his empty e-mail inbox and the cover of her folder, unsure of what to do with himself.

His assistant, Brianna, knocked on the door. Connor closed his e-mail inbox and shuffled Samantha's file to the bottom of the pile as if he had been caught doing something nefarious before calling for her to come in.

"Ms. Cane's assistant called and wanted to confirm your availability for Wednesday afternoon. You had a meeting scheduled for the Stevens-Walker merger, but since you were reassigned," Brianna said the last part under her breath. "I thought I should verify if you were comfortable with the Wednesday appointment."

Conner opened his e-mail again. Still nothing. She wasn't going to bother responding. She had her assistant call to set the appointment. She still wasn't going to talk to him. Connor was instantly enraged.

"Wednesday will be fine," Connor responded curtly, aware and not caring about his own gruffness.

"I'll coordinate to have the rest of the merger team available—"

"That isn't necessary." Connor cut her off. "I will be doing the initial introductions myself." He wanted to minimize the people Samantha could use as a buffer. He was going to force her into meeting with him. He was done being brushed off by Samantha Cane.

CHAPTER SIX

The Reunion

Wednesday morning Samantha spent an hour getting dressed. Despite spending the entire night before trying on every single piece of clothing she owned. Nothing seemed right. She needed something sexy, but professional. She wanted to look both approachable and aloof. Something that showed she was a woman but reminded him of the girl he fell for so many years ago. In addition to all that, Samantha needed it to be understated enough to avoid drawing her colleagues' attention. She didn't want to send the tongues of office gossips wagging with a sudden makeover. It was a tall order for any outfit. Everything seemed inadequate. She felt inadequate.

She spent most of her adult life working on quieting the voice from her childhood. It tormented her, destroying her self-confidence. She built in her mind to keep the voice of doubt locked away. Each achievement in her life, Stanford, law school, becoming a senior associate, was a brick. But, the thought of seeing Connor had it all crumbling down around her. She was that anxious and awkward teenager all over again, standing in front of her mirror, telling herself she wasn't good enough.

She decided finally on a black pencil skirt with a matching blazer. The skirt was a professional knee length, but nearly skintight. It clung to her curves in all the right places, highlighting all the hours she spent on the Stairmaster. The blazer balanced the sexiness of the skirt nicely and made her feel authoritative. The real piece de resistance of the outfit was the red satin blouse, cut just low enough to beg the eyes to linger while still being work appropriate. Barely. Samantha almost never wore red to the office. It was both too sexy and too confrontational. For today, those were exactly the two things she needed to be.

Connor spent fifteen minutes deciding what to wear. He had an extensive collection of personally tailored suits, but he knew exactly which one he looked sexiest in. All he cared about was seeing that familiar look of desire in Samantha's eyes. She might be able to distance herself and avoid him, but she couldn't hide that lingering lust. Connor's suit was jet black and slim fit to show his masculine silhouette. It was paired with a crisp white shirt and a steel blue tie that matched his eyes. The suit itself was lucky. He had yet to fail to close a deal in it, in business or with a woman.

The upside of not being able to sleep was that Samantha got to work almost forty-five minutes early despite how long it took her to get ready. Her meeting with Connor wasn't until two, but she was anxious to get into her office and prepare. Unfortunately, she hadn't been able to focus on anything for longer than five minutes. She kept trying to picture Connor's face, wondering what they years had done to his youthful features. She had Tammy call Connor's office to confirm the appointment, even though it had been set just two days before. She also had Tammy confirm every aspect of the meeting. The conference room. Each team member attending. Mr. Slone was aware. Even the availability of refreshments was confirmed. Still, Samantha couldn't shake her anxiety.

She felt unprepared. She wanted to make sure at no point would she be alone with Connor. If he didn't remember her, it would be easier to hide her devastation with other people to fill the space that had grown between them. If he did remember, she was terrified about what he might say to her if she didn't have some type of buffer. She knew she deserved every angry thing he could want to say to her, but merely imagining the words crushed her. She wasn't prepared to listen to them. Not here, not at her work, where she was supposed to always be in control. She was scared to admit how easily she could lose control to Connor.

She assigned Tammy to meet him in the lobby and escort him into the conference room, something she had never done before. She knew it was mildly rude and unprofessional not to meet him herself, but she couldn't help the little indulgence. She needed to ease herself into the encounter, into being confronted with the full force of his smile, his eyes, his charm, and the raw desire she knew she still had for him.

Connor arrived fifteen minutes early and alone,

hoping to catch her unprepared. He had the exact opposite desire as Samantha. He was determined to get her alone. Although, he had no idea what to do once he did. He wasn't going to pass up the opportunity to find out what would happen between the two former lovers behind closed doors again for the first time in so many years. He was more than a little nervous, but mostly excited and impatient. He was like a man dying of withdrawals and Samantha was his addiction. She held the promise of his salvation while bring his ultimate demise.

He was annoyed when he saw a chubby and cheerful assistant approaching him at the reception desk instead of Samantha. She was still avoiding him, still denying him his drug of choice. Connor didn't have a large ego, but regardless of their history, as a professional courtesy Samantha should have come to meet him.

"Mr. Grayson! Welcome to Phillips, Morrissey & Tanner. Ms. Cane is going to pull Mr. Slone from another meeting and wanted me to show you to the conference room. Is it just you or are we waiting on anyone else?" Her bright smile was small compensation for the insult of not be greeted by Samantha herself. Underneath his irritation, his heart raced uncontrollably at the sound of her name.

Ms. Cane.

He tried to ignore the fact that he was noticeably relieved that she wasn't a Mrs. Was she Ms. Cane because she wasn't married or because she refused to take her husband's name? Samantha was the kind of woman who would never let herself be defined by her husband. He reminded himself that he was getting paid to be here for a reason, and it wasn't Samantha.

He snapped himself back to reality. Connor swallowed his pride and his curiosity, turning the full force of his charm on to Tammy.

"Thank you. It is just me, ready when you are," Connor said through a forced smile. Tammy didn't notice. Connor was too gorgeous, fake smile or not, for anyone to notice the curt undertone in his voice.

"Great. Please follow me," Tammy said as she turned toward the conference room.

Connor followed, taking in his surroundings as he went. Part of his job was to understand the existing environment within a company and to identify early any possible tension points. Despite Tammy's cheerful demeanor, the office itself seemed very stagnant and repressed, more so even than a standard law firm. Connor was immediately struck by the sense that while these people may work well together, they were not a team.

"Here we are." Tammy pointed to a richly furnished conference room. "Can I get you anything? Water? Coffee? Soda?" Tammy rambled a bit while her eyes trailed up and down Connor's fit body, something he was used to, especially in his lucky suit.

"No, thank you…" Connor trailed off while keeping eye contact and smiling at Tammy. Most people with common sense would've realized he was waiting for her name. Tammy was not intuitive in the best of circumstances. With Connor's grey eyes focused on her, she was completely incapable of catching the hint.

I'm sorry. What is your name?" Connor finally asked.

"Oh. I'm Tammy. Ms. Cane's assistant. I'll be just down the hall if you need anything," she replied with a schoolgirl giggle.

"Thank you, Tammy." Connor gave her a quick wink while adding an ounce of sultriness to his voice as he said her name. Tammy giggled again, staring at Connor a bit too long before turning and leaving. From then on, he would be able to get anything he needed from Tammy. It was now five minutes before the meeting and Connor was standing in a conference room by himself, trying to control his growing frustration.

Samantha knew the second Connor was in the building. Although she had been preparing for him since the morning, she was still thrown off by his early arrival. After Tammy had been dispatched to reception to greet Connor, Samantha went to her boss's office to bring him to the conference room. It was completely unnecessary. He knew about the meeting and could find his way to his own conference room. But it was the best excuse Samantha could come up with to avoid being alone with Connor.

To her displeasure, her boss was already out of his office and heading toward the conference room when she met up with him. She was hoping to find him on the phone or at least in his office so that she could distract him with some asinine question to push off having to see Connor for at least a few more minutes. No such luck. With every step closer to the conference room, Samantha's heart began to beat faster. She debated faking a faint. Had her boss not been hard on her heels, she might have. She took one last deep breath before turning the corner and stepping into the conference room. She saw him and froze.

He was alone, but even if the room had been full

of people, Samantha would have only seen him. He was standing across the room, gazing at the city below with his hands in his pockets. He was stunning. Samantha couldn't move. Time seemed to stop as she took in the sight of a grown-up Connor Grayson. He had always been attractive, but all those years ago he was just a boy. Today he stood in front of her as a man.

The sight of him was mesmerizing from head to toe. The afternoon sun colored his chocolate brown hair, perfectly tousled back and out of his face. He was angled slightly away from her, highlighting his strong jaw line while still letting her see the tension in his steely eyes. His shoulders and chest were still athletic and solid. With his hand tucked into his pocket, his jacket rode up enough to let Samantha trace the outline of his firm ass, the sight of which brought a familiar warmth across her body. She was completely unaware of how long she stood in the doorway of the conference room, taking in every inch of his body, until Mr. Slone cleared his throat behind her and tried to push his way past.

Connor turned to face them. An uncontrollable smile lit up his pensive face as his eyes met Samantha's. It was then Connor's turn to take in the sight of Samantha. She would have been happy to know that her outfit choice had its exact intended result. In the few seconds Connor had to trace his eyes over her body, he was both nostalgic for the girl he had fallen in love with and developing new fantasies about the provocative woman standing in front of him. Her skirt instantly reminded him of the one she wore the first time they met, causing an unprofessional swelling in his pants. She was undeniably beautiful. He felt his chest ease as he noted the naked ring finger on her left hand. He was the first to speak as Samantha was still struggling to recover her composure.

"Good afternoon. I'm Connor Grayson with Republic Consulting," he said confidently as he started closing the space between them. He was speaking more to Mr. Slone, seeming aware that Samantha was not entirely in possession of herself. He reveled in the lust she still held for him in her eyes. Mr. Slone held out his hand and introduced himself before Samantha was able to.

"Jeremy Slone. I am the senior partner who will be managing the merger. However, most of the day to day interaction is going to be handled by one of our most capable associates." He shook Connor's hand and both men turned to Samantha.

"Samantha Cane," she blurted out as she shot out her hand to shake Connor's. Connor took her small hand inside his warm and sizable palm. The touch sent electricity shooting through Samantha's body increasing the warmth she already felt across every inch of her skin. Feeling her hand in his reminded Connor of all the nights their hands freely explored each other's bodies. The soft touch seemed to affect both of them deeply. It felt more intimate than a handshake should. Their bodies spoke to each other like long lost friends desperate to get reacquainted. Connor had to resist the urge to bring her hand up to his lips and kiss the inside of her wrist. This simple touch made them both desperate for more contact and yet wary of their abilities to pull away.

If Connor hadn't already noticed how uncomfortable Samantha was by her body language, the growing sweat in her palm as he held it longer than he needed to would have confirmed it. He couldn't resist the urge to torture her further, seeing how far he could push her discomfort. She had ignored him, avoided him, and kept him waiting. Now was his opportunity to make her pay for it, and so much more.

"Ms. Cane," he began in a mockingly familiar tone. "We know each other..." he drew out the words, lengthening her uncertainty. "In a manner of speaking," he finally released her hand while keeping his eyes locked on hers, a wry smile on his lips. Samantha's eyes were filled with terror, a plea for him to stop on her lips, but she couldn't speak the words.

Her eyes shot to her boss, trying to think of a way she could sidestep Connor's comment without giving away her discomfort. She had been scared of what he would say if they were left alone, but now she realized she should have been worried about what he might say in front of her boss and co-workers. No one in Samantha's life had ever known about her time with Connor. In one moment he could change that, spilling their past to the entire firm. Could she explain their past if she had to? She couldn't even admit to herself what Connor meant to her. She would never be able to explain it to anyone else. Luckily, she wouldn't have to. Connor either found his sympathy for her or a greater sense of decorum, before he continued his story. Either way Samantha was thankful his teasing stayed suitable for work.

"We are both graduates of the illustrious Jefferson High School," he said with a knowing smirk. Samantha released a subtle sigh of relief. Reality began to dawn on Samantha that a strange sort of battle had begun between herself and Connor where the winner would be determined by control. He landed the first blow by showing he had power over her based on their intimate past. Samantha was quick to plot her strategy. If he was going to tease, she would ignore. Connor had started this game, but Samantha had too much on the line not to be the victor. This was her office, her boss, her career. She would show Connor Grayson how powerful she still was.

"Right. I believe you were quite the sports star, if I am remembering correctly," she said with a subtlety snide undertone. It earned her a quick wink from Connor that luckily Mr. Slone couldn't see.

"Mr. Slone, I have a shameless favor to ask of you." Connor turned his attention to Mr. Slone, controlling the conversation.

"Is that so?" Mr. Slone asked with an uncontrollable sense of curiosity. Samantha too had no idea what was going to come out of Connor's mouth next. She was trying to prepare her next move, watching their interaction.

"I have been told that you happened to be married to one of the city's most sought after interior decorators. I am going to shamelessly beg for an introduction to your talented wife. I am afraid my bachelor pad is in desperate need of a mature renovation." Connor's playful banter and easy compliments had their intended effect. Mr. Slone was now beaming with marital pride. Connor guessed right that his wife was the best way to endear himself to Mr. Slone. Samantha colored at the word bachelor as her eyes involuntary went to his left hand. She fought the smile that was forming on her lips.

"I will arrange the introduction, but I can't promise she'll have the time," Mr. Slone said with a gentle chuckle. "Like you said, Abby is in pretty high demand. And, please call me Slone," he added with a friendly smile. Slone! Samantha's smile died instantly, replaced with a scowl. She was furious. Mr. Slone had been her boss for three years and she wasn't allowed to call him anything but Mr. Slone or Sir! In less than five minutes Connor already ingratiated himself with her boss. Another point to Connor in their silent war.

"Ms. Cane, I have the rest of the team standing by if you are ready," Tammy chimed in from the doorway, her eyes still noticeably dancing over Connor. Now Tammy was under Connor's power too. Within his first fifteen minutes he won over the two people Samantha worked closest with. He was invading her life, worming his way into the hearts of her colleagues. This office was Samantha's whole world and he already seemed to fit in better than she did.

"Absolutely, let's begin," Connor responded for Samantha, irritating her further by his presumption that he was in charge. But everyone followed his direction. His calm confidence made him a natural leader. People had always gravitated to him, deferred to his judgment. The fact that this was her office and these were her people hadn't changed that. Samantha was beginning to feel vulnerable as the volleys kept coming. She needed to regain the power.

For the rest of the afternoon Samantha and Connor engaged in an unseen power struggle. They were surrounded by people but tussled in a world of their own. They had an unspoken language they used to emotionally joust with each other. Both subtle and cunning, they fought to dominate the conversation, be the center of attention, and earn the interest of those in the room. They struggled to be the one in control

Samantha was losing handedly and it infuriated her. She was determined to get the upper hand before the end of the day. After two hours, the meeting was ending and her time was running out. Connor had listened intently to each of her team member's presentations, asking intelligent questions during each that seemed designed to allow the presenter to display their knowledge. When Samantha tried the same, she sounded accusatory and ended up intimidating rather than motivating.

She wasn't like Connor. He was a genius at making everyone feel important. When he gave you his attention, it felt like you were the most interesting person in the world. Samantha knew that feeling too well. It was intoxicating and right now all her co-workers were getting drunk off Connor Grayson. He was too charming and engaging. She couldn't get the upper hand with all of them fawning over him. If she was going to gain control, she was going to need to do what she had been dreading since she first received his e-mail, really since the last time she saw him eleven years ago. She was going to have to get Connor alone.

Some people were slowly trickling out of the conference room. More were huddled around Connor at the end of the conference table, asking him follow up questions, laughing at his easy jokes, and getting just a few more minutes with his lively personality. Samantha was irked, as she waited for the room to clear a bit. Clearly, she was going to need to be more direct to get Connor alone.

"Mr. Grayson—" Samantha barely began before Connor cut her off.

"Please, call me Connor," his voice dripped with honey. It made all the women in the room melt. Score one more point for Connor. He was winning.

"Connor," she began again with a forced smile. "I have last year's international billing hours for Keiretsu Holdings in my office. If you have the time, I would appreciate going over them with you." Samantha's eyes locked with Connor's. This was what he was waiting for. She couldn't ignore him any longer. He forced her, quite obviously against her initial inclination, to seek out time with him. There was no doubt that she was daring him to be alone with her. Samantha thought if he refused, she would have won. She had no idea she just played directly into Connor's hands. There was no way he would turn down a single moment alone with her.

"I'd love to." He let a touch too much devotion slip into his reply and Samantha's cheeks flushed. Samantha found herself regretting her request and this entire stupid power game. She just overplayed her hand and was headed down a road she could no longer control. Who was she kidding? She hadn't been in control since the second Connor walked back into her life. The only power she'd ever had with Connor was to simply walk away. That was no longer an option unless she wanted to look for a new career.

Samantha led the way to her office, feeling Connor's eyes focused on her ass. The skirt had done its job. Connor's lusty gaze should have made her feel more self-conscious, but instead it did the opposite. Knowing he still wanted her, even if it was just physically, gave her a new sense of confidence. This was how it felt those years ago when she had Connor all to herself, when his only thoughts had been focused on her body and its connection to his. It felt like something was changing between them with each step toward her office, as if they were marching towards something, towards their past and who they used to be. She began to feel more in control. She knew he wanted her.

"Please have a seat." She stood by the door and waved him into her office. He breezed by her, letting his body brush against hers unnecessarily. Samantha tried, and failed, to ignore the familiar flush across her body the incidental touch caused. The only way she could remain in control was if she could keep her own desires in check while forcing him to act on his.

Samantha closed the door behind him, making sure to lock it. She wasn't sure what was going to happen next, but she was sure she didn't want to chance Tammy deciding to walk in. She turned around to see Connor seated in her chair, leaned back with his feet on her desk, a mischievous expression on his lovely face. He had an easy confidence about him that showed her he knew he was winning their secret battle. That was about to change. She wanted him to make a move, reach for her, show weakness, and then she would shut him down. She could push him away and finally take control once and for all.

Samantha strutted over to him. Connor loved to watch that commanding walk of hers. He was starting to get hard just watching her. She stormed right into his personal space, standing next to him behind her own desk as she shoved his feet down to the floor, causing him to rock forward in the chair. He had to spread his knees to either side of hers to avoid knocking into her. He could have moved the chair back, but that would be retreat. He wasn't retreating.

"Go ahead and make yourself at home, Connor," she snarled out at him, taking time to mockingly stretch out his name. He was closer than ever now, touching her, his knees on the outside of her thighs. She could feel her heartbeat racing. She needed to keep control her desires, this was the final battle and she needed a win. But she was losing herself in the sensation of being between Connor Grayson's thighs.

She tried to take slow, deep breaths to keep him from noticing his effect on her. It didn't work. The sound of her deep breaths, almost like panting, was the final straw. Connor couldn't control himself any longer. This wasn't the game anymore. He wanted her. He knew she wanted him. She might be fighting it, but this was going to happen. Connor was determined to have his hands-on Samantha again. Right now.

He stood up without backing up, dragging his body against hers as he rose. His hands traced the outside of her legs from her knees to her thighs, sliding under the hem of her skirt. Samantha leaned back against her desk to keep from falling over as she was overcome by a desire for him. Her mind continued to struggle to tell her body she didn't want this. This wasn't the plan. There was no planning when it came to Connor.

"Don't mind if I do, Samantha," he whispered against her lips. The familiar feeling of his hands on her naked thighs made her wet instantly. But it was when she heard his sultry voice, that she knew there was no point in fighting. Her mind had lost, her body had won. Connor had won. He was in control. She wanted him and he knew it. Samantha slid her hands up his arms, resting them on the back of his neck and pulling his lips to meet hers. The kiss they shared contained eleven years of cravings. It was frantic, passionate, demanding, and even angry. They wanted each other and hated themselves for it.

Connor pushed aside her panties, sliding his fingers inside of her wetness as he slid his tongue into her eager mouth. It was happening so fast because it had taken so long.

"Is this what you want?" His words took them back to their first tumultuous meeting.

"Yes," she panted out as his thumb began to circle her most sensitive area and his fingers drove deeper into her.

"Tell me you want me," Connor commanded her. He wanted her, but he needed to hear her say it. Now it was his turn to be in control, his turn to make her confess her desires and then leave her wanting. He wanted her to say the words out loud. He wanted the satisfaction of knowing she admitted to wanting him so she couldn't deny it ever again.

"I want you." She was lost in the sensations his body and words were creating.

"Tell me you need me." He was pushing her. She refused to need anyone. He wanted to hear her say she needed him or prove he could walk away when she didn't. He would be the one to walk away this time. This was payback.

"I need you." Samantha didn't think before responding. It was true. Her body needed him. She didn't want him to stop. She was close to coming.

Connor was shocked. Even like this, when she was

at his mercy, seconds from coming, he didn't think she would admit to needing him. Until that moment, he had planned on walking out on her, getting her to admit she wanted him and then leaving her to drown in that want. Now, she admitted it so easily, so quickly, so freely. He wanted to push her further. He needed to know if she would say it.

"Tell me you love me." Connor's voice dropped to a barely audible whisper in Samantha's ear. The intimacy was enough to push her over the edge. She couldn't think. She couldn't speak. All she could do was feel the wave of pleasure he caused burst across every inch of her body.

"Connor...I...I...I'm coming," was all Samantha could say as her body shuttered with ecstasy. Connor was angry. Not because Samantha didn't say it, but because he let her come without saying it. He should have walked away. Yet again he gave her what she needed without getting what he wanted.

"Yeah, I didn't think so," he spit out at her as he walked around to the other side of her desk. Samantha instantly regretted the loss of their intimacy, an overwhelming sense of vulnerability swelling inside of her. His words, combined with the sudden loss of their physical connection, cut Samantha deeply. She had an aching want for the warmth of his body and the soft caress of his whispered words from moments ago. She slid off her desk and pulled down her skirt, suddenly excruciatingly unsure. She turned to meet his eyes and drew back at their sudden resentment.

"I'm too old for this school yard shit. Either let me take you to dinner, and we do this thing for real or..." Connor was struggling with what the alternative was. He wanted to be with her, but not like this. Not like before. Not behind closed doors, in secret. He wanted all of her. He wanted her to want all of him. "Or, we're done. I'm not doing this again with you."

Through the shock and confusion of the sudden change in him, Samantha heard the defeat in his voice and it broke her heart. This wasn't a game anymore. Somewhere along the way it had become real. She should have known things between them were never a game. Whatever connection they had, it had always been real. Connor's eyes remained locked on her, waiting for an answer.

"I don't date co-workers," was all Samantha could think to answer. She was so confused about what he wanted, what she wanted, and what she could give him. He laughed spitefully at her, a sound that sent a chill down her spine.

"You're right. It's much more professional to come all over my fingers in your office than to let me take you out to dinner." His words slapped her in the face with her own lack of control. No one had ever made her feel as ashamed as Connor did in that moment. She was stunned. She couldn't speak. She couldn't even look at him. She bit the inside of her cheek as hard as she could. She refused to let him see her cry.

"Then, I guess that's it." When he got to the door, he turned back to her. She was still frozen behind her desk, not wanting him to leave, but unable to think of what to say to make him stay. She felt like she gave him everything she was able to give and it hadn't been enough. She wasn't good enough for Connor. The voice was right.

"For old time's sake, Elsie. You're welcome." Her heart ached at the sound of her nickname, but he didn't bother looking up at her.

And with that, Connor Grayson left Samantha Cane standing alone in her office with a sense of complete emptiness in her heart and a look of complete confusion on her face.

CHAPTER SEVEN

Moving Forward

Connor stormed out of Samantha's office, furious. He didn't respond to Tammy when she bid him a friendly goodbye or wave back at the handful of other people he met that day. He couldn't bring himself to go through the motions. He knew that his cold exit was burning some of the good credit he built earlier, but it was unavoidable. He couldn't bring himself to make eye contact with anyone. He didn't trust himself not to snap on the next person who was foolish enough to try to talk to him. His only concern was to get out of that office and away from Samantha as soon as possible.

She had done it to him again. She rejected him. She got what she wanted out of him and then tossed him aside. He couldn't believe he let her get to him again. He knew better. He wasn't an eighteen-year old kid anymore. He knew what he wanted. This time he was audacious enough to ask her for it and she said no. She wouldn't even have dinner with him! He was such an idiot. He should have known. He should have kept his distance.

Connor stepped into the elevator and smashed the button for the lobby a dozen times, not caring that he was going to crush it. He wanted to break something. Smash something. Destroy something. The entire drive back to his house, all he could focus on was how angry he was at himself. His temper was barely in check. Fury burned through his veins. He felt it singe his heart. It was a miracle he stayed on the road. He threw his keys down on the end table in his entry way, dragging his hands through his hair and letting out a deep breath. Then, he threw the entire end table against the wall, watching the wood splitter into a million pieces with weary satisfaction.

"Fuck!" he shouted as every muscle in his body tensed in pure rage. He walked to the bar and poured himself a double whiskey. He finished it in two large gulps before pouring another and slumping down into his couch. He was utterly exhausted. He felt destroyed. He replayed the entire day with Samantha in his head. Everything aside from her office had gone better than he hoped. Everyone in her office was in love with him. Everyone, except the one woman he wanted since he was eighteen.

Connor thought about what to do next. His first instinct was to call Rebecca and get off the account. She wouldn't let him. He was sure of it. She already lost her patience with him trying to avoid taking it last week. She wasn't going to be more inclined to let him off after an initial meeting which by all accounts—except his—had gone well. He could lay out his entire history with Samantha. That was the only way to begin to explain what happened in her office. Connor would rather quit than explain how Samantha Cane rejected and destroyed him. Again. The upside to the secrecy that Samantha always insisted on was his humiliation was just between the two of them. Connor was keen to keep it that way.

He could quit, but he liked his job. He would have to quit effective immediately to be sure he wouldn't have to see Samantha again. If he did, Rebecca would not only refuse to give him a reference, she'd go out of her way to keep him from finding a new job. He would probably be looking for a new career. As much as he wanted to avoid seeing Samantha again, he wasn't willing to sacrifice his entire life to do it. Connor sipped his second double whiskey, coming to grips with the fact that he was trapped. He was going to have to keep seeing Samantha.

As the whiskey began to filter into his blood, he began to calm down. He replayed each interaction with Samantha. He knew the look on her face when she saw him in the conference room. She was trying to hide it, but she felt something for him. He was sure of it. Maybe it was just lust, but Samantha wanted him physically at least. The fact that he was so well received with her colleagues really annoyed her.

The more everyone else liked Connor, the more Samantha wanted to control him. That was the reason she asked him to her office to begin with. He made the mistake of giving in to his own desires when they were alone, but before that he was in complete control. Samantha was the one part of Connor's life where he couldn't trust his instincts. For the first time in his life, he was going to have to make a plan and stick to it.

As much power as Samantha had over Connor, he was the more charismatic of the two. He had more general appeal, was more well-liked. If he was going to have to keep seeing Samantha, those were going to be his two weapons: her lust and his charm. He wasn't going to run. He was going to fight. He was going to make sure everyone in that office couldn't get enough of him. He was going to spend as much time around Samantha as possible, ensuring she could see how much her officemates pined for him. He wouldn't let them cross that line again, he wouldn't be alone with her. He would keep her wanting him by not letting her have him. A sense of peace began to settle on Connor as he developed his new battle plan to conquer Samantha Cane.

Samantha on the other hand had no idea how to act the next time she saw Connor. She followed him but stopped at the threshold of her office. She had no idea what to say to him and she certainly wasn't going to make a scene in front of the whole office. She had a million emotions swimming around in her head and needed time to process them. She had Tammy hold her calls and sat in her office, trying to make sense of what just happened. At first, the ruling emotion was shame and disappointment. She had never felt ashamed of being with Connor before, but his words made her painfully aware of how impetuous she was. She let things go too far. She couldn't help herself. No one had been able to make her feel the way Connor did. She had a handful of lovers in the eleven years since Connor took her virginity. None of them could compare to the way she felt when Connor touched her. It was exactly the way she remembered it. It felt like their bodies were made for each other, his hands designed to touch her. She had given herself to him eagerly and without question. For that, he mocked her.

Shame began to give way to indignation. He instigated their tryst. He had no right to make her feel guilty for giving in to him when he was the one leading her, pushing her. He made her confess she wanted him. She needed him. He made her come. Then, he had the audacity to get angry with her for not giving him more. She still wasn't sure what he wanted. Did he really expect her to say she loved him? She had never said those words to anyone other than her parents. He was angry she wasn't willing to go on a date with him, but their history was too confusing, too painful. Their connection was too unpredictable to bring into her work.

The reasons she walked away from him all those years ago were still as real as they had ever been to her. They were why she never had a serious relationship. They were why she didn't have close friends. They were why she was so alone. She couldn't need anyone. She always had to be able to walk away.

Working through her whirlwind of emotions, Samantha came to a resolution. She needed to keep as much distance as possible from Connor. She couldn't give him what he wanted and she couldn't control herself if he got too close. Their relationship would have to stay completely professional.

Distance was going to be nearly impossible while working on the merger. Samantha debated asking Mr. Slone to take her off the team. She could find some excuse that he would probably accept. Her caseload was too heavy. She wasn't sure she was prepared.

None of that worked with her thirty-year plan. This was her ticket to making partner. She worked hard and wanted it bad. She couldn't walk away now just because Connor was standing between her and her goal. She would've to work with him. The only way to do that would be to keep her distance physically and emotionally. She refused to let herself be drawn into anymore battles or office rendezvous.

Connor and Samantha once again had opposite objectives for their next encounter. Samantha wanted distance, Connor wanted anything but. Their wills would be tested sooner than either would have liked.

CHAPTER EIGHT

Take Two

Connor came to work the next day with a wide smile and a light step despite the hangover causing a throbbing in his temples. He brought donuts, another one of his simple tricks. He had yet to work in an office where free pastries weren't appreciated. It was a cheap way to earn him bonus points, to show he was happy to pay his way into their good graces. He didn't have an office, so he spent the first hour or so of the morning in the break room. He sipped his coffee and initiated casual chit chat. He often learned the most about an office and the people in it from the offhand chats. People were much more willing to share secrets when they felt they were "off the record". Connor always found that in general people liked to talk if you were able to make them feel comfortable. That was Connor's specialty, making people feel like he was their best friend from the first meeting.

In his hour in the break room Connor learned that Samantha was feared at Phillips, Morrissey & Tanner. People acknowledged she was a hard worker, but they were all aware her dedication was self-motivated. The perception was that she had no loyalty. Connor wasn't surprised by any of it. He saw the same side of Samantha all her co-workers did, the distant and cold woman who was so focused on achieving her goals she lost sight of the people around her.

Even without their past, the fact that Samantha was handling the merger without the support of her co-workers was going to make Connor's job more difficult. People always got nervous during a merger. Change is always disruptive. Connor's job was to keep everyone calm and working happily toward a common goal, something he knew was much easier if the team believed in the project. If people didn't believe in Samantha, they were going to have to believe in him.

Connor finished his coffee and his reconnaissance before heading over to Tammy's desk. The time he spent chatting with her yesterday was going to pay off now. Normally he would coordinate through his counterpart, but in this case that was Samantha. Not only was she likely going to be combative with him, she wasn't well trusted by her staff. He was going to work around her and take control of the transition team. The fact that he knew leading the team was going to drive Samantha crazy was a bonus, but not his primary motivation. Or, so he kept telling himself.

Connor confidently strolled up to Tammy's desk, making sure he kept eye contact with Samantha's assistant and a playful smile on his lips. He came around to her side of the desk outside of Samantha's office, leaning against it effortlessly while he gently encroached in her personal space. He was close enough Tammy could smell his musky cologne. Connor knew Samantha was in her office. Getting close to Tammy was both to avoid having Samantha hear him and to keep Tammy off balance while he used her to undermine Samantha as the merger team lead.

"Good morning, Tammy. How are you this fine morning?" Connor asked the smitten assistant.

"I'm good, Mr. Grayson." Tammy blushed.

"Oh gosh, please call me Connor." He flashed his sweet smile and watched her let out a nearly inaudible sigh.

"Is there something I can do for you, Connor?" She met his eyes when she said his name, drawing it out in an unnecessarily intimate way. The poor girl had no chance. She was going to give Connor whatever he asked for. "Do you want me to let Ms. Cane know you are here?"

"Oh, I don't think there is any need to bother her. I'm sure you can help me with everything I need." Flattery was one of Connor's favorite tools. "My team is going to be coming in here shortly and as of right now, we don't have anywhere to work. Could you help me reserve a conference room?" He knew this was a small task, clearly within Tammy's purview.

"Oh sure! I can do that." Tammy was only too eager to help. She clicked through her computer for a few minutes before looking back up at him. "You are all set for conference room two," she announced with pride.

"Perfect. You are a lifesaver." Connor was just getting started. "Now, is there any place I could make a few phone calls? My own office would be great, but I totally understand if there isn't enough space for me..."

"Um. I'm not sure..." Tammy was hesitant. Office space was at a premium in the building and it was above Tammy's pay grade to decide who got to occupy one. Connor pressed her. He could work out of his office at Republic Consulting, but that wasn't going to get him anywhere with Samantha.

"I know it is a lot to ask. It's just that I am going to be here so much, you'd be saving me from having to make a trip back uptown to my office at the end of every day. I'd be in your debt forever." Connor poured on the charm mercilessly.

"Let me make a call," Tammy cooed, eager to be Connor's hero. She picked up her phone and started playing her own game.

"Hi Sandra. It's Tammy. Look I've got a huge favor to ask of you. I need an office space to steal for the next few weeks. I didn't submit a space usage request, but you know how you-know-who gets—" Tammy gave a sideways glance at Connor who looked away, pretending like he wasn't listening. He was sure she was talking about Samantha. Tammy was more cunning than he gave her credit for, leveraging camaraderie of shared suffering. Connor chuckled at the thought that Samantha was a team builder in a way.

"And if I don't get this fixed, I'm going to be toast." Connor couldn't hear the other end of the line, but it was good news based on the look on Tammy's face. "That's great! Sandy you are the best! Thank you so much. Next round at happy hour is on me!" Tammy hung up with a wide smile and victory in her eyes.

"You can have Mr. Simon's office. He just retired and they were waiting to refurbish before re-assigning it. It is empty, but there is a desk, a computer, and a phone. I can show you were it is," Tammy announced eagerly.

"That would be lovely." Connor stood up and motioned for her to lead the way. Tammy directed him to a large office on the other side of the building with a beautiful view of the city. This was obviously a partner's office. Connor smirked thinking how much his working out of this office was going to infuriate Samantha.

"Will this do, Mr. Gray...Connor?" Tammy corrected herself.

"This is absolutely amazing, Tammy. Thank you." Connor rewarded her with another smile as he rounded the desk. "One last thing, could you send out a meeting notification to the team for this afternoon? I want to introduce the two teams. We'll be meeting in Conference Room two at eleven," Connor said with enough confidence Tammy didn't question.

"Will do, Connor," Tammy said with a smile as she left the room. Connor was left alone in his new office, a satisfied smile on his face. His coup was well underway.

Samantha spent most of the morning sequestered in her office. She knew Connor was in the building and was desperate to avoid seeing him. It was easy to bury herself in merger paperwork. It wasn't until she got an appointment alert at eleven that she ventured out of her office.

"Tammy, what is this eleven o'clock appointment on the calendar? I didn't set any merger team meetings for today," Samantha asked her assistant.

"That is the meeting that Connor scheduled this morning. He said he wanted to introduce the two merger teams," Tammy replied with a hint of surprise in her voice.

"Connor?" Samantha was stuck on the familiarity of Tammy's address.

"Yes. Mr. Grayson. He asked me to schedule the meeting this morning. I assumed you knew about it," Tammy explained genuinely confused.

"No. I didn't know he scheduled the appointment. Tammy, please ensure you confirm with me before scheduling any appointments or meetings." Samantha tried to control the annoyance in her voice. While she was irritated with Tammy, she was furious with Connor. There was no use in screaming at her misguided but well-meaning assistant.

Samantha stomped over to the conference room. She wasn't happy that she was going to be blindsided by Connor's meeting, but it was better to go unprepared than let him have a merger team meeting without her. That would be tacitly accepting he was the team lead. He wasn't. She would oversee the merger team. This was her key to becoming the youngest partner at Phillips, Morrissey & Tanner.

Connor was standing at the head of the conference room when she walked in. He looked just as amazing as the day before in his crisp, custom tailored suit. It seemed like he had just begun to address the room when Samantha walked in. She stood in the back with her arms crossed. He stopped mid-sentence when he saw her and smiled despite her scowl.

"Samantha, glad you could join us. Please come in and sit down. I was about to tell the team what the keys to a successful merger are." His tone was soft and friendly. To anyone but Samantha, he seemed entirely genuine. But she knew better. He was taunting her. First, he was highlighting she had been late to an appointment he intentionally set without her knowledge, using her own assistant to do it. Second, he insinuated he was the only one who knew how to lead a successful merger, trying to make her feel insecure. Finally and most importantly, he was clearly highlighting the fact that he was in control. He was the leader now. She fumed silently, refusing to listen to the voice in the back of her head echoing Connor's subtext.

"How lucky I found out about the meeting in time," Samantha couldn't help from quipping back at him across the packed conference room. She regretted it the second she said it. His comments sounded welcoming. Hers sounded bitter and juvenile. Another point to Connor. They were back to playing the game. How did they get back here so fast? Samantha took a deep breath and reminded herself to be professional and distant. Don't let him bait you, Samantha!

"Okay. Now, where was I?" Connor looked around the room, easily regaining his momentum.

"Integration," a soft female voice offered. Samantha turned her eyes to the right side of the conference room to where the voice had come from. It was Jessica Winters. She was a petite blonde who worked in the accounting department. She was sitting right next to Connor, close enough to almost touch him. Jessica's body language said she was riveted by what Connor was saying. She had her notepad on her lap, leaning in toward him, biting her lip softly in anticipation. Or, maybe it was desire. Samantha was positive Jessica knew all too well her position gave Connor the perfect angle to see down her shirt.

Samantha only interacted with Jessica a few times and always thought her work was acceptable. Not now. Right now Samantha hated Jessica. It wasn't the first time she had seen women look at Connor with lust filled eyes. She was never been jealous before when she knew Connor was hers. Now it was different. The force of Samantha's anger caught her off guard as she struggled to appear composed. Professional. Distant. It was Samantha's mantra. She repeated it to herself over and over again as she bit back the envy and spite.

"Thanks, Jessie." Connor gave her an approving smile, setting his hand on her shoulder for only the briefest of seconds. Jessie?! It was bad enough he had the whole office calling him Connor, now he had pet names for the women she worked with! They met yesterday. There was no way they be so familiar. Professional. Distant. What do you care who he smiles at, Samantha?

"Integration," Connor continued. "Our ultimate goal is for two companies to become one. While that may sound simple, it is a very intricate process that at times can be trying even in the most beneficial of mergers. Agreeing to a merger is like falling in love with someone."

Connor's eyes were instinctively drawn to Samantha. Their gaze locked for a moment. She felt their connection in that fraction of a second. It was still there, that magnetic draw that brought them together years ago. "It is easy and feels good. You are both so excited and think the other can do no wrong."

Samantha was the first to break eye contact, afraid he would see how flustered his stare could make her. Of course he did. He could always read her body.

"Actually merging two companies, now that is like moving in together. Suddenly, someone else is in your space, telling you how to fold your towels, what drawer the silverware should go in, taking up half the medicine cabinet with God knows what, and insisting the toilet seat should always be put back down." Connor paused for the laughter to subside.

Even Samantha had to admire how easily he commanded the room. A feeling best be described as sentimental endearment flooded her. The warmth lasted only a moment before one simple thought rocked her world. Was Connor speaking from experience? Had he lived with someone? Did he currently live with someone? Samantha convinced herself it wasn't possible, not after the way he touched her yesterday. Samantha couldn't picture Connor in love with someone else. The mere thought made her heart ache. She knew she could never have Connor, but the thought of him belonging to someone else almost broke her.

"There are a million tiny things that you don't think about when you agree to move in with someone. They can sour the experience and make you forget why you fell in love in the first place. The important part is to see past those growing pains, keep your eyes on the future, and remember that each side will have to compromise a little. Integrate your lives, just like we need to integrate these two businesses. So, how do we do that?" It wasn't a rhetorical question. Connor was actually asking the group for ideas. An awkward silence fell over the room which made everyone nervous. Everyone except Connor, he still had a smile plastered on his confident face.

"Come on people, I know you are all clever. Let me hear some of your ideas. What do we need to do to integrate?" His voice was encouraging.

"Coordinate billing practices?" Jessica's hesitant voice rang out. A twinge of hate trickled down Samantha's spine at her words. Samantha reprimanded herself for the childish backbiting and reminded herself to be a professional.

"Yes! Exactly, Jessie," Connor praised.

Samantha's mouth filled with that familiar metallic taste, but she managed to choke back the audible huff lingering in her throat.

"We need to be on the same page when it comes to billing practices, but more than that we need to align our entire business model," Connor was putting words in Jessica's mouth, giving her credit for his ideas. This was another tactic Connor used regularly. Reward the first people who spoke up, make their answer the right answer regardless of what they say. Encourage ideas and cooperation to create a real team.

"More than just our billing practices, we need to align all of what we do. Staff structure, the systems and processes we use, the products and services we provide. These are all things that form the basis of what our new company is going to be. What else?" Connor looked around the room again, encouraging more answers.

"We'll need to make sure our clients are comfortable during the change," another young associate offered up. Connor was equally enthusiastic with this answer.

"Yes. Thank you, Justin." Connor knew everyone's name. Samantha didn't. He was already more a part of the office than she was. "Secure our client base. Our clients are going to be nervous, right? Things are changing and we need to reassure them that we are still just as committed to taking care of all their needs. Furthermore, our client base is expanding into a whole new continent. We need to be flexible to the demands of a new clientele, in a whole new language! What else?" This time there was hardly a pause before Connor got another answer.

"Build a new logo?" another associate chimed in from the back.

"Good. A new logo. What is the significance of a name and a logo? That is our brand, right? That represents who we are and what we stand for. We need to maintain our brand recognition throughout the process as we integrate and form a new fused company." Again Connor was taking a simple idea and expanding it to fit what he wanted everyone to see. He had a knack for making people feel appreciated and special. Samantha wasn't surprised. Connor always made her feel that way.

The next time he asked, there wasn't a pause before Connor got more answers. The collaboration continued for another fifteen minutes with Connor giving each person credit for having the right answer, making each feel like they had a completely new and unique insight as Connor tied their idea back to his three tenants.

"Let's recap. The most important thing we are trying to do is to integrate two companies into one.

We are going to do this through aligning business models, securing our client base, and maintaining our brand recognition. Excellent work." Connor looked around the room, making eye contact with each associate like a proud parent. "Each of you has been specially selected for this transition team because of the unique skill set you have. You are all experts. I need you each to take some time, think about the objectives we have outlined here today and how your section can contribute to this effort. We'll meet back here tomorrow at the same time and discuss a way forward. Thank you, everyone."

And with that, everyone began to shuffle out of the conference room, except Connor and Jessica. Jessica was talking to Connor in an obviously flirty way, tilting her head to the side, giggling, and brushing her hair behind her ear. Connor casually leaned against the table, his muscular arms tensed as he used them to prop himself up. Samantha didn't realize she was staring at them until Connor glanced back at her. She instantly snapped her eyes away, turning to one of the associates leaving the room, asking him about some random report she was vaguely familiar with. She continued to babble to this associate, while giving sideways glances to Connor and Jessica. Her mantra was worthless. She wasn't professional or distant. She was incapable of tearing her eyes away from Connor and Jessica, watching them lean in, smile, exchange incidental touches. She couldn't stop herself from coveting the intimacy of their innocent flirtation. When she saw them both walking together toward the door, she had to intervene. She had a desperate desire to have all of Connor's attention again.

"Connor, I need to speak with you," Samantha called out to him in a cold and detached tone as he and Jessica were just about out the door. The words were out of her mouth even before she could think of a lie to follow them. Connor and Jessica stilled, both slightly caught off guard by the abruptness of Samantha's interjection. It was clear she was going to need to provide more before Connor was going to acknowledge she'd said anything at all. Everything was a power struggle with him.

"I have some concerns regarding the local labor laws which may impact the staff alignment and we need to discuss them." She intended it to be a direction, ordering him to her office. Connor dismissed it like an asinine request.

"Jessie and I were just heading out to lunch to brainstorm some billing solutions. Would you care to join us?" Connor's invitation was a taunt. Samantha wasn't going to compete for his attention.

"I already have a lunch engagement," Samantha lied.

"That's too bad. Marcus is our labor expert. I will have him swing by your office this afternoon to discuss your concerns." Connor's voice was both warm and dismissive. He was blowing Samantha off and she could barely contain her rage.

"Shall we?" Connor said to Jessica, his hand on the small of her back as he gestured out the door. "Enjoy your lunch, Samantha," Connor called back to her, a wide and wicked smile on his lips.

Samantha spent the remainder of her afternoon in her office, fuming. Connor flat out refused to speak with her. She was the senior associate on the merger team and he was treating her like anyone else. Less than anyone else! He was strong arming his way into the office and no one seemed to care but her. She told herself her anger was based on being pushed out of the merger and not being pushed out of Connor's attention. She tried to ignore the voice ringing in her ears.

That is kind of girl Connor wants.

Simple, easy, open, sweet.

The kind of girl you will never be.

The next morning Samantha was poring over the financial reports Jessica submitted. She never spent so much time reviewing these reports. Today she was determined to find an error. The only problem was there didn't seem to be any. She was walking back to Jessica's desk to return the reports with her begrudging approval when she saw Connor. He was leaning against her desk in his casual way and Jessica was giggling at something he said. When she reached out and stroked his forearm, Samantha lost it. She stormed over to Jessica's desk and slammed the report down in between them, physically breaking up the two, and almost crushing Jessica's hand.

"These are completely wrong!" Samantha towered over Jessica, nearly shouting in her face. Jessica was too stunned to respond. "What were you thinking?"

"What is the problem, Samantha?" Connor's voice was sterner than usual, but still steady as he tried to intervene.

"The problem, Connor, is it seems Jessie is too busy laughing at your jokes to do her job," Samantha spat out, her voice laced with venom. She hadn't intended on making a scene, but at this point she was unable to control her words and was too enraged to realize how far her voice was carrying.

"I completed the weekly reports the same way I always do," Jessica meekly replied trying to defend herself.

"Exactly. Are we doing business the same as we always do? No. We are in the middle of a merger." Samantha was aware she wasn't entirely making sense. Her brain was trying to work out where she could go with this to avoid looking foolish. She hated every word that was coming out of her mouth. She hated who she had become, the catty, jealous office bitch. How did she get here? How could she get back to who she was? Why couldn't she control how she felt about Connor?

"I am sure Jessica is more than capable of making the changes you need. In the meantime, can I speak with you Samantha?" Connor gave a reassuring look to Jessica while grabbing Samantha's elbow and leading her back to her office forcefully. Samantha pulled away from Connor's touch, blaming him as much as herself for her outburst. She practically jogged back to the safety of her office, running from the sound of Connor's quick steps behind her and the humiliation she felt growing in the pit of her stomach. A wave of nauseous passed over her as she braced herself against her desk. She had overstepped her bounds and the entire office had seen it.

Connor stepped into Samantha's office behind her, closing the door. She faced away from him, her hands on her desk with her head down in defeat.

"What the hell was that?" Connor's voice rang out in the empty space between them. "You looked like a crazy person out there!"

"I know," Samantha's reply was so soft Connor almost didn't hear it.

"I'm trying to build a team here and in five minutes you manage to ruin all the progress we've made," Connor admonished. Every word cut Samantha deep, not only because they were true, but because they were coming from Connor.

"I know," Samantha's voice was a little louder now. Connor could hear the remorse in her words.

"You know these people are terrified of you! Scenes like that don't help."

"I know. I know! I KNOW!" Samantha turned around to face him. The passion and sadness in her eyes shoved aside every thought in his head other than the desire to hold her. He checked it quickly, not letting himself cross that imaginary line. Connor suddenly realized for the first time they were alone in her office again. Less than two days ago he promised himself he wouldn't put himself at risk and here he was, alone with Samantha Cane.

"You think I'm not painfully aware of how hated I am and how loved you are? You win okay. Now can you stop rubbing my face in it!"

"What are you talking about?" Connor knew exactly what she meant, but he wasn't going to admit it. He suddenly felt guilty. He shoved his hands in his pockets to push down the urge to touch her and tell her he was sorry.

"Don't play innocent. It's bad enough you're taking over my entire office, but to be flirting with Jessie, right in front of me," Samantha used a mocking girlie tone when she said Jessica's name

"And why shouldn't I? We are both single consenting adults. Just because you've made it very clear that you don't want to date co-workers doesn't mean I won't." Connor was defensive. They both knew there was something between them, whether she admitted it or not. She didn't get to deny it and throw it in his face at the same time.

"Because you are driving me crazy!" Samantha confessed with an exasperated sigh. She didn't mean to say the words out loud. She hadn't been able to admit them yet to herself, but they were said now. And they were true. It was making her crazy seeing him with someone else, even if it was just a simple office flirtation. Connor was taken aback by her sudden confession and didn't respond. "Can you please just stop?" Samantha whimpered in defeat.

"Why should I?" Connor chided, always wanting to push her.

"Because I'm asking you to." Samantha's eyes were pleading.

"Why does it bother you so much? You made it clear you aren't interested." He knew exactly why. But he wanted her to admit it. She wouldn't. She just glared at him with a look that accused him

"Samantha, I have the right to date whoever I want. You are not my boss and you sure as hell aren't my girlfriend. You have no right to tell me who I can flirt with. Who I can date. Who I can kiss. Who I can fuck..." Samantha cringed with each word until she couldn't take it.

"Then I need you off this project," Samantha snapped. Her mind was swimming with images of Connor with someone else. They felt like jagged shards of glass rattling around, slicing through her ability to think rationally.

"That's not going to happen," Connor retorted with anger rising back in his voice, overtaking the sympathy he felt a minute ago. She wasn't chasing him away again. This was his job and she'd have to deal with it.

"Connor, I can't work like this."

"Well, you don't have a choice. Neither of us does. Believe me when I say that I did everything I could to avoid seeing you again. I didn't want to do this job to begin with and you certainly haven't made it any more pleasant." Connor's words were pointed, but honest.

Samantha's only response was to cradle her face in her hands and let out a muffled scream. She looked up and her eyes met Connor's again. In that moment they both silently acknowledged they were trapped together and it was painful for them both.

"Fine," Samantha said with resignation taking a step toward him. There was still half an office between them, but that single step felt like the beginning of something, like the ground was shifting under them

"Go to dinner with me." She was left with no other choice. She didn't want to date Connor, but she couldn't get away from him and she refused to watch him with someone else. She was out of options.

"Excuse me?" he teased with a cautious smirk.

"You heard me, Connor." Her voice was a warning not to push. He didn't listen.

"Are you asking me out on a date?" He was painfully playful now. Samantha refused to smile in her defeat.

"Yes." She walked around to her side of the desk trying to regain at least the perception of control. "Pick me up tomorrow night at seven. I'll make dinner reservations." Again she was trying to order him around. He might be forcing her into this, but she would at least control what she could.

"Tomorrow is Friday."

"Yes. I am aware of that Connor. That is what usually happens after a Thursday." Sarcasm dripped from her words as she stared at him. Her hands were on her desk and she was leaning in. A power pose.

"You're assuming I don't have plans." Connor crossed his arms, bathing in her frustration.

"Connor, can't you please be graceful in victory?" Samantha was equal parts defeated and defiant. She was faking the confidence, trying hard to make sure Connor didn't see her trepidation.

"Victory? I haven't said yes yet," he continued to tease her. He had no intention of letting her back out of the invitation, but he loved seeing her squirm.

"Well, I'm sure Jessica is still at her desk if you'd rather. Well?" Samantha was at the end of her rope. Connor let silence fill the room until he felt the anxiety radiating off her.

"I'll see you tomorrow at seven," he finally retorted. "Wear something sexy," were his parting words before strutting out of her office. Samantha was sure he intentionally said it loud enough Tammy could hear.

Maybe Thursdays weren't so bad after all.

CHAPTER NINE

The First Date

Wear something sexy. His words rang in her ears as Samantha stared at her closet Friday night. What do you wear on a first date with the boy who took your virginity and was now a stunningly beautiful man who makes you come unhinged? Samantha couldn't decide what she wanted from this date. Or, more importantly, what she wanted from Connor. Her plan to never be alone with him failed. Twice. The first time she felt the delicious touch of his hands on her skin again. She missed that feeling every day, but it ended in a flaming mess. The second time, she let herself get trapped into this date. Both were categorical failures.

She needed a new strategy, but first she had to figure out what she wanted. Could she keep Connor at arm's length until the end of the merger? If she didn't, could she indulge in his touch and keep herself from falling for him? Was it possible to be in Connor's arms and not want to spend the rest of her life there?

She asked him out after being cornered, pushed to the edge of reason. She wanted to cancel at least a hundred times since he left her office, working herself into a near panic. She knew she couldn't back out, that he would push his relationship with Jessica even further if she did. Now that Connor knew her weakness, he would be merciless. She knew he could be viciously determined and singularly focused. It was part of why he was an amazing lover. When he was with her, he was only with her. The rest of the world didn't exist. It was hard enough to focus just knowing Connor was in the office. If he was flirting with Jessica every day, in every meeting, Samantha knew she would snap again. She hated herself for it, for that primal jealousy that took over from some barbarian part of her brain, but she knew it was true. When it came to Connor she was never in control. She always acted on instinct, without the ability to be rational. So much for distant and professional.

Samantha was still staring at her closet, time ticking away until Connor would be knocking on her door. Conflicted didn't even begin to describe how confused she was. She wouldn't admit to herself how badly she wanted to have Connor's naked body pressed up against hers again. She kept telling herself to be careful, to make sure he didn't fall in love with her. Again. She would have to try to be friends with Connor. Not even a friend, a work colleague. No emotional attachment. She couldn't let it get physical or one of them would get hurt. The idea of being with him, but not being with him felt impossible.

She thought about wearing her office clothes and pretending this was a work dinner, professional as possible, nothing but a firm handshake at the end of the evening. Her traitorous fantasies responded by picturing Connor's face as she answered the door in nothing but a sexy lace bra and panties. She unconsciously smiled at the thought of never even making it out of her apartment. She glanced at the clock and chased the fantasies away with her ensuing panic. Connor was going to be at her door in an hour and she was still standing around in nothing but her underwear. Finally at a total loss and nearing hysteria, she broke down and called Monica for some much-needed girly advice.

Monica had been Samantha's best friend since their senior year. They went to different colleges and lived in different cities, but they always kept in touch over the years. Everyone else from both high school and college seemed to just fade away after graduation. Monica was the last woman standing, the only person to ever put up with Samantha's bullshit. Even before her father died, Samantha was never a barrel full of laughs, always a bit prickly. After, she added being emotionally distant to the list of her finer qualities. She was hardly a prize. Being her friend was always difficult and often unrewarding.

She never tried very hard to keep friends and put zero effort into making them. The more people she let in, the more she had to lose. You can't miss what you've never had. Samantha was happy with the distance she kept from the rest of the world. Through both college and law school, Monica had been the only person she really talked to. They didn't talk regularly, but any time Samantha called it was as if no time had passed at all. Monica didn't get mad when Samantha went radio silent for months on end. She gave her space, content to know they were friends and always would be, regardless of how often they talked or how deep their conversations went. Samantha set the phone on her dresser and listened to the rings on speaker, still pulling items out of her closet and tossing them aside in disappointed disgust.

"Hey bitch! To what do I owe the honor?" Monica was irreverent, one of her most endearing qualities in Samantha's opinion. It was impossible to hurt Monica's feelings, probably the main reason she was still friends with Samantha.

"Nice to hear your voice too, wench. Don't freak out alright, but I need your advice." Mocking banter was part of their status quo.

"Holy shit! You're knocked up!" Monica screeched into the phone.

"No! Jesus…"

"Right, you'd have to knock boots to get knocked up." Monica couldn't control her laughter, thinking she was just too clever. It flooded through the phone and filled Samantha's bedroom.

"Fuck you."

"You wish."

"Urgh. Why do I even bother?" They were both laughing now. A little bit of the stress that racked Samantha's body all day eased out of her shoulders.

"Fine. What profound wisdom can I bestow on you tonight then?" Samantha took a deep breath, steeling herself for the confession she knew was going to earn her some vulgar teasing.

"I have a date." Other than an exaggerated gasp, Monica was completely silent. "With Connor

Grayson." Samantha braced herself against her closet door, preparing for the questions she didn't want to answer.

"Well, fuck me sideways."

"Such a lady."

"Not all of us have that fancy courtroom etiquette training. Tell me, is he as sexy as I remember? As built as he is in my wet dreams?"

"Scorching. I have no idea what to wear tonight. Ergo, the phone call."

"Nothing. Wear. Absolutely. Nothing. Let him ruin you. You need it." The thought of being ruined by Connor Grayson made Samantha's thighs clench involuntarily.

"I can't! It's complicated." Samantha didn't know how to explain. Monica didn't know about her history with Connor. No one did. "We are working together."

"So? What does that matter?"

"I hate mixing work and pleasure." Samantha let out an exasperated sigh and covered her face with her hands. Monica wasn't helping and time was still ticking off. She was friends with Samantha long enough to know there was something more going on. But she also knew when not to push. There was no way she could force Samantha to confide in her if she didn't want to. Some best friend.

"Fine. So, what is the look you are going for then? What do you want him to think when he sees you?" Samantha took a minute to think. She asked herself the same thing all day and couldn't quite put her finger on it.

"Sexy, but classy, I guess."

"That's easy, the LBD," Monica declared as if

Samantha was a complete idiot for not thinking of it herself.

"LBD?"

Little black dress. I swear you live under a rock."

"Just trapped behind a desk. Plus, people our age usually don't speak in acronyms! What are you twelve?"

"These calls are so rewarding. I love being able to help you out…" Monica was teasing, but Samantha still heard the warning in her tone. She was close to hanging up and letting Samantha figure it out on her own. She grabbed a black cocktail dress from the back of her closet.

"Fine. I'm a dick. Sue me. What else? Make-up? Hair? Up-do or down and free?" It was as close to an apology as she ever gave Monica, but it was enough.

"Keep the make-up natural, nude lipstick, small bit of blush, understated smoky eye shadow, but lots of mascara. Make sure he sees when you are batting those bad boys at him. Hair definitely down. Curl the ends just a bit and then run your fingers through it so it looks like you aren't even trying."

"Brilliant. Accessories?" Samantha plugged in her curling iron and dug out her mascara.

"Simple studs for earrings, but something long and dangly that will hang between the girls all night making him stare. I'm winking, but you can't see it."

Samantha giggled as she dug through her jewelry box, pulling out a long chain necklace.

"Shoes?"

"Hmmm. That's a tough call. You want to be work friends, simple black flats. You want him to fuck you so hard you can't walk tomorrow? Red stilettos."

"Got it. I've gotta get ready. Thanks, you little

minx. You're a lifesaver!" Samantha's gratitude was sincere.

"Anything for you, hussy. Send me a picture when you are done so I can admire my handy work!"

Samantha was dressed and applauding Monica's fashion tips as her eyes turned to her still bare feet. She pulled out both the ballet flats and heels while she was getting ready, trying to decide as she got ready. They were still sitting at the end of her bed torturing her when Connor arrived. He was a few minutes early, but he didn't come to the door. Instead Samantha's phone buzzed with a text.

Connor: I'm out front. Ready whenever you are, beautiful.

Really, a text? Apparently, Connor wasn't much of a romantic. Samantha let her mind wander to images of how their first date would have been half a lifetime ago, back when he loved her. A twinge of regret twisted her stomach before she brushed the daydreams away. She slid on her shoes, shot a quick picture to Monica, and rushed downstairs for her date.

"I know this is a business dinner, but seriously a text? You couldn't be bothered to come to the door?" She didn't even say hello before starting in on him. It was going to be important to set the tone early tonight. Connor needed to be clear she was here because she was being forced, not because she wanted to.

"First of all, this is a date. Not a business dinner. And honestly? I didn't trust myself to be alone with you that close to a bedroom." His words were laced with lust. He wasn't joking. Samantha blushed, wondering what he would have thought of Monica's nothing-at-all outfit option. She derailed that train of thought, wiping her sweating hands on her thighs. Her phone buzzed with a new text.

Monica: Nice stilettos slut ;)

A smile crept across Samantha's lips as she put her phone away. She looked over at Connor, unprofessional thoughts swimming in the pool of desire that flooded her mind. His eyes were locked on the road and her smile faded. Despite racking her brain for something safe to say, the car ride was awkwardly silent. It seemed like they were both unreasonably nervous. The car reeked of fear by the time they arrived at the restaurant.

Samantha chose a middle of the road restaurant, nothing too romantic but deciding against the local burger joint. It was a quaint mom-and-pop Italian place fancy enough to have cloth linens. Connor smiled in approval when they were seated.

"This place is nice. I thought maybe you'd end up taking me to a sports bar or something to keep from having to talk to me," Connor said with a chuckle.

"I thought about it, believe me. Especially since there's a game on tonight." A small amount of the tension was fading as the initial ice broke. Samantha wanted to stay professional, but she couldn't stand the idea of continuing the painful silence of the car ride for an entire dinner. Especially now that she was seated across from Connor, being forced to face him instead of mindlessly staring out the car window.

"A game?" Connor inquired.

"Game three of the series with the Jays."

Samantha knew he was aware of what game she was talking about.

"I didn't know you liked baseball."

"You never asked." Her response was flat.

"You weren't big on talking if I recall." He sounded more defensive than he meant to. The awkward silence was back, drowning them both in waves of regret. Him for current comments, her for past actions.

"I guess you're right about that." She had a pensive pause, almost long enough to make Connor apologize for bring up their past, for insinuating she was anything other than exactly what he wanted. "I guess we have some catching up do to do." The guilt for how Samantha had treated him was fresh in her mind. She tried to make her voice light and playful. "Yes, I like baseball. I used to watch your games. You know that summer—" they shared a knowing smile— "I mean, when I wasn't in debate and the crowd was big enough you wouldn't notice me." A flush of self-consciousness washed over Samantha at her confession.

"Really?" He was honestly having trouble believing her. How could he not have noticed her? Even if she was trying to hide, he could spot her from a mile away. He knew every inch of her body and there was no one else like Samantha Cane. Connor momentarily caught himself wondering how her body changed as she became a woman. He colored at the thought of her naked. He tried to focus back on their conversation, on her confession. Connor realized he never saw her because he never looked in the stands during games. One-hundred percent focused. That was how he did everything. The thought of her watching him brought a smile to his lips and new warmth to his heart.

"I never knew you watched me," he said with a soft smile on his lips. The tension was falling away with every word.

"You weren't supposed to. Breaking the rules, remember?" she quipped with a seemingly apologetic smile.

"What else don't I know about you?" He ignored her reference to their past. He wasn't going to let himself think about it. How she always kept him at arm's length. How she broke him. How she left him. This was a new day. A new them. A new chance. He wasn't going to let their past get in the way.

"Everything, I guess. What do you want to know? Ask me anything." Openness was Samantha's penance for her past. He knew he could ask her anything and she would answer honestly.

Why did you leave me? Did you love me? Could you ever love me?

His heart was desperate for the answers, but his lips refused to ask the questions. Don't live in the past. Don't push her away. His heart ached as he tried to think of any question other than the ones he couldn't speak.

"Let's see, I already know where you grew up and how you take your coffee." He forced himself to sound cheerful. "What about your favorite color?"

"Guess." Samantha was feeling playful.

Connor thought back all the years he'd known her, all the outfits she'd worn, the color of her room back home. There was never really one color more present than the next. He had absolutely no idea.

"Red." He took a stab in the dark.

"Close. Pink." She buried her face in her hands, stifling the words as if it was a shameful confession. He laughed out loud at her shyness.

"You never wear pink!"

"I know. I hate that I love it. If anyone asks, I usually say green. Nice neutral green." When she pulled her hands away from her face, her blushing cheeks were the most beautiful shade of soft pink. It was Connor's new favorite color too.

"What's wrong with pink? I like pink," he said, loving how the blush on her cheeks deepened.

"It's so soft. So girly." She spat the words out like she was allergic to them.

"Well, last time I checked, you are a girl." A naughty smirk crossed his lips and Samantha couldn't help herself from laughing out loud.

"First of all, I am a woman," she puffed out her chest for emphasis. "Secondly, women can't afford to be soft in this world."

"You mean corporate law?" he asked, genuinely curious.

"I mean sure, there especially, but everywhere. The world likes to see women as damsels in distress, needing to be helped along or taken care of. Whether guys admit it or not, I have to try harder to prove that I'm capable because of it."

"I don't think anyone mistakes you as a damsel in distress." He meant it as a compliment. Connor thought back to the image of her the first day they met, in front of that classroom, looking like she was born to command the world's attention.

"Of course they do. All the time! Like when I try to put my suitcase into an overhead bin, or check my oil at the gas station, or God forbid I try to buy something from Home Depot without seeking the advice of every man in the store!"

"Come on. They are just being nice." Connor hadn't meant to end up arguing with her on their first date, but it seemed like that was where the conversation was heading.

"Would they be that nice if I had a penis?" Samantha realized she said the word a bit too loud as shocked faces turned towards them from around the restaurant. She and Connor both giggled slightly at the stares she got in response.

"No, they wouldn't. They are trying to save the damsel in distress and I sure as hell don't need saving. I am just as competent and capable as any man." She took a breath, realizing by the startled look on his face that she'd been ranting at him for longer than first date etiquette should allow.

"Anyway, that's why I don't wear pink." She leaned back in her chair, feeling like she'd soured the short break in awkwardness they enjoyed.

"I guess I never thought of it like that," Connor contemplated while running his finger through his hair. "You've just always seemed so"—he searched for the right word— "Forceful. It honestly didn't occur to me someone could make you feel otherwise." Samantha's heart melted at his words

"Oh yeah? Why were you surprised I liked baseball then?" Her voice was mocking, but sweet.

"Maybe because all the nights we spent together, you never once asked me about it. And I thought you never came to my games," was his teasing reply.

"Well, I wasn't big on talking, remember?" She used his words against him with a knowing look in her eyes.

"Touché. So, pink. Good to know."

They managed to struggle through some cliché first date banter as they waited for their food, letting silence fall while they ate. It wasn't the worst date Samantha had ever been on, but it was certainly one of the most bizarre. They were hot and cold. There were glimpses of how easy it would be to fall in love with him followed by a painful stiffness that made her want to run away screaming.

She was relieved when the night was nearly over and Connor pulled up outside her apartment. He parked and quickly jumped out to open her door. She hid her smirk at his gesture and decided against making a joke about damsels and door handles. She took his hand as she got out of the passenger seat and he pulled her into him, toe to toe and chest to chest. He wrapped his other hand around her waist and Samantha let out a soft gasp of surprise, unable to pull away. She avoided even incidental contact the whole night and now she let herself end up in his arms.

"Thank you for a lovely evening." His lips were on hers before she was able to argue about the loveliness of the night. Samantha was in utter shock. Connor Grayson's lips were pressed softly to hers again after eleven years. Her whole body tensed, but he didn't stop.

She felt his fingers on her hip first, tickling the faint line of her panties under her dress. Then they began their slow trace up her waist, slowing at the side of her chest as if debating a detour to her nipples. Instead they continued up her body, along her exposed collar bone, causing goosebumps to break out across her body. His fingers continued up her neck and brushed along her jaw line until his hand was cradling the side of her face, tilting gently to deepen their kiss. She finally snapped back to reality and her body took over, the way it always would with Connor. She wrapped her arms around his neck and pulled him closer to her.

Connor's soft kiss turned passionate and desperate. Standing on the sidewalk outside of Samantha's apartment they kissed like they were trying to make up for the lost years. Samantha's tongue pressed into Connor's mouth and he let out a soft groan. Both arms were now wrapped around Samantha's waist like he was trying to squeeze her into him and keep her forever. Samantha's body responded by continuing to lean into him, causing them to stumble back into Connor's SUV. He was pinned. The old Samantha was coming back now, the one who dragged him into the girl's bathroom and ravaged him. His kiss flipped a switch in her and she was pure carnal lust. She moaned as Connor's hands roamed her body, never letting her lips leave his. She could feel their mutual arousal electrifying the air.

With no warning, Connor's lips broke from hers as he pushed her arm's length away. She glared at him in amazement.

"I need to leave now if I am going to keep this night PG," he explained. He looked as tortured with desire as she was.

"And why do we need to be PG?" Samantha tried to take a step back toward him, desperate for the warmth of his body pressed against hers again. To hell with professional and distant. She wanted to take him upstairs and rip his clothes off. He kept his arms up, keeping her at bay.

"Because I'm not that kind of guy. You don't get past first base on the first date. I want to be wooed," he simpered. He leaned in, kissed her forehead and quickly retreated to the driver's side of car. "Gotta keep you wanting that second date, right?" he quipped with a wink before starting his car and driving off.

Samantha watched until his car disappeared down the street, trying to make sense of the last few hours. They had such an awkward date, but then that kiss. It was more than a kiss, that was a full on make-out session. She hadn't been kissed like that ever. At least not since the last time she kissed Connor. Then, he just drove off. How was that even possible? She knew he wanted it just as much as she did, but he was able to hold back. Samantha spent her entire weekend trying to decipher her first date with Connor. Come Monday morning, she was nowhere closer to understanding what was happening between them.

She hoped seeing him again would clear up where they stood. The look in his eyes, the tone of his voice, if he was avoiding her, would give her some clues as to how he felt about her. Samantha was excited and anxious to see Connor again.

CHAPTER TEN

The Rules

Eleven years ago...

Samantha stared at her computer screen, desperately willing herself to start researching her next debate topic. Her mind wouldn't cooperate. All she could think about was Connor. It was a few days since their last rendezvous and she hadn't seen him. Or more correctly, she hadn't been seen by him. She made a point of walking by the field at the end of her debate class every day to secretly watch him on the field during his practices. Watching him seemed to calm her. She always went home with a smile on her face. But they hadn't had any more secret bathroom rendezvous. Part of her was relieved

How many times could you fool around in a high school bathroom before getting caught? She was too clever to throw away her chance at Stanford by getting caught having sex in a bathroom!

She was a virgin and had never really thought about sex, at least not like that. It was something she knew eventually would be part of her life. But when she thought about sex. It was just something you did. It had never been an enticing idea for her. After Connor that changed. Her mind raced with thoughts of being with him, connected to him in the most intimate way. For the first time in her life she wanted it. She wanted to have sex with Connor. The realization made her flush.

The only problem was either he was intentionally avoiding her or was simply too busy to bother. She wasn't sure which one she would rather. She didn't seek him out either, but she wasn't avoiding him. Maybe he thought it was her turn. Was that how it was going to be, they took turns finding each other when they needed it? She wanted to be with him again, but it couldn't be in the school. The last two times were spontaneous and passionate, but they were also stupidly risky. She knew her parents were heavy sleepers and their room was at the other end of the house. If she waited for him at the back door, he could easily sneak into her room. Samantha shook the thoughts out of her head. Was she seriously thinking of how to sneak a boy into her room? That was insane. Debate topic research. That's what she should be doing. Her mind didn't seem to listen as it kept plotting.

How could she get him to come over? She could try to catch him alone at school but based on their history there was a good chance they would end up in another bathroom again. That didn't solve her problem. She didn't have his phone number, so she couldn't call him. Their school had an on-line messaging system that a lot of kids used. It was supposed to be for school projects, but everyone used it to chat during class because phones weren't allowed. It was possible that he still checked it, even though he graduated. It was worth a shot. Worst case scenario, he wouldn't get the message and she'd be in the same position she was in now.

Samantha: Do you ever use this?

She waited for twenty painful minutes, obsessively clicking back and forth between the chat window and a research page, trying to fool herself into believing she was getting work done. It was already eleven o'clock at night. Maybe he had gone to bed. Maybe he didn't check his messages. She was about to give up when that beautiful chime hit her ears. Her heart began to beat faster at the thought of Connor's fingers typing out a message just for her.

Connor: yep.

That was it. She waited twenty minutes for three letters followed by a pompous little period. She wanted to scream. Was he going to participate in this conversation at all? She was so nervous. She wanted to talk to him so badly, but now that she could she had no idea what to say to him. Did he even know who she was? They never actually met and it's not like they exchanged names in between passionate kisses.

Samantha: Do you know who this is?
Connor: yep.

If Samantha could reach out and choke him through the computer she would. Just another three letters. He certainly knew how to torture a girl. He was going to have to say more than that for her to keep going.

Samantha: Prove it. Who am I?
Connor: the girl who thinks i'm a lucky charm

Samantha's face lit up. There were a million ways he could have answered, some of them less flattering to her than others, but he chose to remember her nickname for him. She took a deep breath and thought about what to say next, fighting back the butterflies in her stomach. There was no point in asking how his day was. They weren't dating. They weren't even friends really. Get to the point, Samantha.

Samantha: are we going to keep doing this?
Connor: what?

Samantha came close to throwing her computer out of the window. Was he intentionally being difficult?

Samantha: You know what.
Connor: our bathroom rendezvous?
Samantha: Yes...those

The moments that ticked off before he responded were agony for Samantha. Why was it so important that he said yes? She was desperate for him and wanted to know he wanted her. Someone like Connor wasn't really the dating type. Besides, he was going off to college in a couple months. There wasn't a future between them. This could only ever be a fun summer fling. Before Connor, Samantha would have laughed at someone suggesting it. Now, she would take any time with Connor she could get.

Connor: played the best game of my life after last time. looks like we're both lucky charms

Samantha wasn't sure if that was an answer or he was just bragging.

Connor: yep...i'm game to keep going
Samantha: Okay. Fine.

Samantha was trying to stay aloof and dispassionate despite feeling exactly the opposite. Connor couldn't help shaking his head and laughing at the fact that she spelled out okay. Who spells out okay in a chat message?

Samantha: But we need to be smarter. NO MORE BATHROOMS! We're going to get caught.
Connor: k
Samantha: I think we should have some ground rules too.
Connor: rules?

Guess it shouldn't surprise him that she was a control freak. She'd been in complete control each time they'd been together. It didn't bother Connor. On the contrary, her strength was one of the sexiest things about her. Most people in Connor's life deferred to him to make decisions. There was just something about him that made everyone look to him for answers. He seemed to always end up in control, be it his friends or the girls chasing him. He was used to it mostly, but it got exhausting. He craved someone who would tell him what to do for a change. He craved Samantha.   .

Samantha: Rule 1. This is between you and me. No bragging to buddies.
Connor: didn't realize I was something to brag about, but I appreciate your discretion ;)

A winking face? Really, Connor? Are you a twelve-year-old girl? Samantha would have gagged if it weren't adorable. Focus Samantha! Set ground rules so you don't end up falling in love and getting your heart broken.

Samantha: That also means no public displays of affection, no winking, no sexy smiles, no hidden looks. To the rest of the world, we are just Connor and Samantha.
Connor: the rest of the world? i'm something else to you?

Samantha didn't know how to answer that, so she didn't. She completely ignored his question and pushed on with the rules she needed in place to protect herself. She wasn't stupid enough to think that someone like Connor Grayson, who had the world eating out of the palm of his hand, wanted to seriously date her. She was convenient. She didn't need more.

Samantha: Rule 2. No obligations. We aren't dating. We don't do dinner. We don't do cuddling. We don't ask how the other's day went. In fact, least amount of talking is best.

That rule stung a bit. Connor knew Samantha was smarter than he was. He didn't take the advanced classes she was in. He did fine in school, but focused on sports not grades. He was going to UCLA on a baseball scholarship, not because of his academic achievements. She was making it clear that she didn't want him for his witty conversation. He wasn't her type. Connor swallowed his pride. This was going to be a casual summer fling. He could deal with that, if she wasn't with someone else.

Connor: Rule 3. No dating other people. I'm not a cheater. If either of us is with someone else, this stops.

It was a good rule, but Samantha's stomach turned at the thought of Connor with someone else. He couldn't be clearer about the fact that she was a good way to kill time until he found a girl he wanted to date.

Samantha: Agreed. Rule 4. I can change my mind any time. It doesn't matter if I ask you to come over at 2 a.m. I'm not a tease, but if I change my mind when you get here, no objections.
Connor: who the hell do you think I am?!?! i'm not a fucking rapist!!!

Samantha felt a twinge of guilt. She hadn't meant it like that. She just wanted an escape hatch in case she wasn't as brave with him in her bedroom as she had been in the bathroom.

Samantha: Sorry. I didn't mean it like that. I mean no

guilt trips or blue ball comments. Whoever initiates the meeting is in control.
Connor: you mean you'll pretend I'm in control
Samantha: Don't worry, Lucky. I'm a great actress. ;)

Cheesy smiles were on both of their faces. As much as they tried to deny, there was something special between them. In some way, they just fit.

Connor: 6565554798
Samantha: ???
Connor: my number. next time just text me

Less than a minute went by before Connor's phone buzzed.

Samantha: 62 Rainier St. Come to the back door (not an innuendo!!!). Text me when you get here.

Connor's heart felt like it was going to beat right out of his chest. He typed L.C. into his phone to save her number, his lucky charm. Then deleted it and typed "Elsie" chuckling at his new secret code name for her. He put on his shoes and was out his front door in less than ten minutes.

CHAPTER ELEVEN

The First Time

Eleven years ago...

It had been about three weeks. Three amazing, unforgettable, life-changing weeks. That chat conversation opened the floodgates. They were both intoxicated with each other, addicted to their time together. It was exhilarating. They still hadn't had sex, but they spent nearly every night together. At least, they spent several hours each night with each other. Even if sleepovers hadn't been against Samantha's rules, they weren't smart. Sneaking around at night was risky enough. A sleepover was just asking to get caught. Samantha wasn't keen on explaining to her Dad why he found a boy in her bedroom.

The nocturnal rendezvous meant that Samantha was chronically sleep deprived. She regularly sacrificed her sleep to study or prep for a debate, but she wasn't big on sacrificing sleep for pleasure. It was exchanging short-term rewards for long-term suffering. It didn't make sense. Feeling tired kept her from being on top of her game. She was the standout in her debate class, but she knew she wasn't giving it her all. She could be better if she got even just a few nights of decent sleep in a row. She would spend each day telling herself that she wouldn't text Connor. She would stay home, alone, and just sleep. Then, each night she would maniacally check her phone, waiting for a text, eager to send one herself. She always needed one more fix. She had no self-control when it came to Connor. They alternated regularly between his house and hers. At first, she refused to initiate two nights in a row, afraid that she would be asking too much or he would say no. He never said no. He was always quick to respond, like he was waiting on her text, just as eager as she was. She could tell he was tired too, but he always seemed happy to see her. As tired as she was, she always left Connor feeling refreshed and relaxed.

Most nights went similarly. In accordance with the rules, they never really talked. They might have a few witty comments back and forth along the lines of "funny meeting you here" and "long time no see", but they never went deeper. They never let themselves get too attached. The second the door was closed and they were alone together they would spend at least twenty minutes kissing, sometimes soft and slowly. Other times, in a painful fever. Another half hour was spent slowly exploring each other's bodies. It wasn't exactly cuddling. It was more active than that. It was almost a form of intimate worship. They took turns tracing the peaks and valleys of each other's bodies with fingers, lips, and tongues, slowly peeling clothes off each other until they both ended up totally naked. Samantha had the same body image problems every girl has. But she never felt self-conscious with Connor. He spent so much time kissing every inch of her reverently, it was impossible to think there was a part of her that he didn't adore. By the end of the night at least one of them would always climax. Usually, they would both find a release. After three weeks, they were very familiar with the first three bases and even rounded third on occasion as they kissed naked in bed.

Samantha could kiss Conner forever. She could tell what kind of day he had by how he kissed. It was the opposite of what she expected. When he was happy his kisses were frenzied, no thought in his head other than the feel of her mouth on his. When he was upset, he was almost too gentle to believe, like his lips were directly connected to his heart.

Two days ago, she watched his team lose a practice game. They didn't just lose, they were destroyed, getting beaten by double digits. Connor struck out twice and missed a catch that let a runner advance. It was a small error, but the anger was written all over his face. At the end of the game he kicked his batting helmet against the wall of the dugout, almost cracking it. It earned him a verbal lashing from his coach in front of the whole team. Samantha had never seen him so furious. It scared her. She made up her mind to give him space. She hadn't expected to get a text that night based on the mood he was in. She was wrong. Just after eleven o'clock, her phone chimed and the name "Lucky" popped up on her screen.

She made her way over to Connor's, not sure what to expect. In the past he had been passionate, but never rough with her. She was scared he would be now. Would he take his anger out on her body? Quite the opposite. He was unimaginably tender. When she stepped into his room, he took her hands in his and interlaced their fingers. He kissed her forehead and each of her cheeks before pressing his lips softly to hers. It was like a plea, a desperate entreaty to accept him. Each kiss made her feel how vulnerable he was, a glimpse into his own self-doubt. He was disappointed, frustrated, and dejected. Each kiss broke Samantha's heart.

She wrapped her hands around his waist to pull his body against hers and hugged him tightly, trying silently to tell him everything would be okay. She was here for him. He wrapped his arms around her shoulders and buried his face in her hair returning the sweet embrace. They stood in his room, locked in their first hug, surrounded in a calming quietness. As always, their bodies said the words their mouths never could. It felt like they were each giving a piece of themselves to the other, making each other whole with their acceptance. The intimate serenity brought tears to her eyes, emotion overwhelmed her. They were both fully dressed and yet were more connected and vulnerable than ever before.

She let him pull away first, making sure he knew she would be there for him if he needed. Once he stepped back, she felt they crossed some unspoken line. Their normal routine of fooling around didn't seem appropriate anymore, but she didn't want to leave him. Breaking the rules, she asked him if he was okay. He claimed it was just a bad day as they stood together in silence. She held his hand in hers as she led him to the bed. Without a word, he knew to lie down beside her.

They laid together cuddling for hours, listening to the sounds of their hearts beating together. They were connected in an intangible way that brought them both a sense of peace. Just as silently, they got up together and Connor followed Samantha to the door. She had given him exactly what he needed. She was just there, existing with him. He kissed her one last time gently before she left for the night.

That was two days ago. They hadn't seen each other since. Two nights was the longest they had gone without seeing each other in three weeks. Samantha was too nervous to text Connor. He was vulnerable with her and somehow, they slipped into an emotional connection. She tortured herself for the past two nights, still not sleeping, wondering if he regretted being vulnerable in front of her. Was he uncomfortable with the new type of intimacy they found together?

Connor was nervous he broke her rules and pushed her away. They weren't supposed to be together like that. Cuddling wasn't allowed. Samantha didn't want a relationship with him and yet he called her when he needed someone. He had friends he could have called and talked to, who a month ago he would have. Now, she was all he wanted. It was a horrible day and all he wanted was to hold her. That night they both realized what they have was more than either of them was ready for. He was scared she was avoiding him, but he didn't want to let her just fade away.

Lucky: come over at ten
Elsie: I'm not sure my parents will be asleep by then.

Lucky: parents took my sisters to a softball game out of town. have the house to myself tonight. come over.
Elsie: I'll come over as soon as I can.

Samantha's heart soared when she saw the text from Connor. When he said they would have the house to themselves the whole night, she started to get nervous. She wondered if he was thinking they would finally have sex tonight. She waited for the sound of her parents going to bed. It was somewhere just before eleven when she texted Connor that she was on her way.

Connor's house was only about a fifteen-minute walk from hers, less on nights she was so excited to see him she practically jogged. Tonight was the opposite, she was dragging her feet and second guessing herself. Her fear wasn't about having sex with Connor. She felt safe with him. It felt right for him to be her first. She even started birth control after their first night together, just in case. It was just that voice in the back of her head again, the self-doubt, that made her nervous.

You are a clumsy virgin.

He is going to laugh at you.

This is when he finally figures out you have no idea what you are doing.

She tried to push the voice aside as she kept her feet moving her forward. She had been with Connor dozens of times now. He had seen all of her, touched all of her. It was just sex. What was the big deal?

Because you are going to be bad at it.

Samantha did a quick u-turn, heading back to her house as she pulled out her phone to text an excuse to Connor. She was on the verge of a full-on panic attack. She stared down at her phone, trying to think of an excuse she could send him. They never cancelled on each other before. It felt like a weird form of betrayal to lie to him. Samantha took a deep breath, put her phone away, and turned back toward Connor's house. This was Connor. There was nothing to be afraid of. After about three more stops and starts, she finally made it to his house about a half hour later.

Sneaking into Connor's room was extremely convenient, almost like his parents didn't care if he had girls over. His family had four kids and he was the only boy, so he took over the converted garage with its own door to the outside. If he left the side gate unlocked, she could walk right into his room from the street. The first time she knocked on the door softly like she was there to deliver a pizza or something. Connor had teased her and told her to just come in.

Each time since then he was waiting just inside for her. This time he wasn't. Samantha looked around Connor's empty room and noticed his bedroom door was open. It was never open. Connor must have gone to grab something from another room in the house. Samantha stood awkwardly in the middle of Connor's room, waiting for him to come back. After a few minutes went by, she started to inch toward the open door, peeking out around the corner. Connor said that his parents and sisters were going to be gone, but she still didn't want to go strolling through the house in the middle of the night like she owned it.

"Connor? Connor?" She took a tentative step outside the room and called out softly to him. There was no response. She sent a text asking where he was.

She thought about going back home for a second before she heard a loud laugh echoing through the house. She heard Connor giggle before when she accidentally tickled him, but she never heard him laughing out loud like this. She followed the sound down the hallway. Connor was standing in the kitchen wearing nothing but his boxers, eating ice cream out of the carton, and laughing at something on his phone.

"And what is so funny?" she called out to him from the doorway. She was hoping that she would surprise him enough to make him jump. Instead, he just calmly followed the swing of her hips as she strutted up to the kitchen counter and stood next to him. His eyes said he approved of the button up dress she that hugged her curves and fell to her mid-thigh.

"Finally! I thought you were never going to get here!" was his snarky response, but she knew he was excited to see her.

"Calm down. It's only eleven thirty!" she teased him back as she hopped up on the counter, knowing it would hike her dress up and drive him crazy. "So, what were you laughing at?" Talking was breaking the rules, but it felt comfortable in a way it hadn't before. And she loved the sound of his voice.

"Watch this," he started giggling again as he handed her his phone. She laughed out loud as she watched the video of a small puppy disappear into a snowbank, just a wagging tail poking up from the whiteness. Muscled, sexy, manly Connor was laughing out loud at a cute puppy video. Samantha's insides melted. A text message alert popped onto his screen from a girl named Elsie. A spike of jealousy shot down her back. She knew she shouldn't read it, but she couldn't help herself. It was her text, the one she sent from his room a minute ago. He gave her a nickname.

"Elsie?" she held up the phone to show him their chat history.

"Yeah. Lucky Charm. L.C. Elsie," he replied with a prideful smile, taking back his phone. "Why? What am I saved as on your phone?"

"Lucky. With a little four-leaf clover icon." She looked away, blushing with the juvenile confession.

Elsie and Lucky. I like it. Like we're spies or star-crossed lovers or something." His mouth turned up in a sexy irresistible smirk.

"Come here." She wrapped her arms around his neck, pulled him between her legs and kissed him. It was cold and sweet. "You taste like strawberries," she giggled into his lips.

"Try some," he said as he pulled away from her a little but stayed anchored against her hips. He fed her a spoonful of the strawberry ice cream, relishing the happy moan she let out at the taste.

"Yummy. So, this is what you do when you have no adult supervision? Eat ice cream in your underwear?" she teased as he continued to alternate feeding them each bites of ice cream.

"Of course, this is my perfect night. Nothing but me, some ice cream, and my beautiful woman." His words were sultry. Samantha barely had time to register that he called her beautiful before realizing he called her his woman. Her heart was so full. She loved the sound of it, despite the mild misogyny. Still, terror filled her veins. So many rules were getting broken, so many walls crumbling.

"So I'm your woman now?" She was trying to

sound light and playful, but her voice came out shaky and insecure. Connor set down the ice cream and slid his arms around her waist.

"Well, I'm yours, so I guess I just assumed you're mine too." His eyes locked on hers with a questioning passion. Samantha couldn't even respond. She just grabbed him and pulled him to her, kissing him deeply. The kiss was all the answer he needed. He wrapped her legs around his waist as he lifted her off the counter and carried her back to his room. He sat down on the edge of his bed, pulling her down on top of him, her lips never leaving his. Samantha knew she wanted to make love to Connor tonight.

"This is my first time." She didn't need to explain. He knew exactly what she was talking about. They never talked about having sex before, or the fact that she was a virgin, but somehow, he knew. She pushed away and stood in front of him, far enough that he could see all of her. Slowly, she pulled her dress over her head and let it drop to the floor. She reached behind her, unhooked her bra and let the straps slowly slip off her shoulders before she pulled it off and dropped it next to her dress. Connor let out a ragged breath, staring at Samantha in just her panties. She nodded to his boxers. He caught the wordless direction and slipped them off to the floor, sitting completely naked on the bed, eyes locked on Samantha's. She hooked her fingers into the sides of her panties at her hips and slid them down her body painfully slowly.

Connor had seen her naked before, but never like this. He had never been able to take in her entire naked body, knowing he would soon be inside her. She let his eyes dance over her body, building anticipation before she climbed back into his lap, straddling him on the bed. She rocked her hips and suddenly their bodies were aligned, seconds from coming together. He wrapped his arms around her waist, keeping her from being able to sink down onto him. Samantha was confused and looked down into his eyes for an explanation for his resistance.

"This is my first time too," he confessed, his lips tangled with hers.

"Good," was her only reply. She was surprised at his words, but happy at their meaning. She would be his first and whatever else happened between them, he would never forget her. He eased his grip on her waist and she let herself slide down onto him, feeling him fill her completely. There was a sharp stab of pain marking the fact that she was no longer a virgin. It quickly faded in the warmth of his arms. He reached his hands up her back, gripping her shoulder and cradling her head as she slid up and down his thickness. Their bodies were connected, forehead, chest, and hips. Their lips tickled each other as they took ragged breaths together.

It felt better than Samantha thought it could. It wasn't awkward or scary. She was in control but giving herself to him completely. The feeling of Connor filling her entirely, over and over, hitting places inside of her she never knew existed was pure ecstasy. Hearing his hungry moaning, knowing she was the cause, thrilled her. His arms helped guide her as she sped up her motions, coming down on him faster and harder. Knowing he was close to coming was exhilarating.

"Come inside me," Samantha's words triggered Connor's release instantly. He held her tight as his body shook with pleasure. His final wild thrust pushed her over the edge and they came together. Exhausted and completely spent, he collapsed back into his bed, taking her with him. They scooted up the bed, so they were both able to relax. Samantha was resting on his chest, entranced by the steady sound of his racing heart, a heart that was now forever connected to hers. They were cuddling again, this time with their naked bodies intertwined. Samantha couldn't help herself from breaking her own rules. It just felt so right. They were both asleep within minutes, bodies tangled together in a satisfied peace.

Samantha woke up first. Brushing the sleep from her eyes she saw a still sleeping Connor underneath her.

I love you.

The uncontrollable thought invaded her mind unprovoked and unexpected. She was in love with Connor Grayson. Completely. Utterly. Stupidly. In. Love.

She panicked. This wasn't supposed to happen! She jumped out of bed, away from Connor, like the distance would make it less true. Connor began to wake up as Samantha hurriedly got dressed.

"Connor wake up! We fell asleep." She was already halfway dressed as he reached out to look at the time.

"We still have time. I can give you a ride to school." Sleep was still thick in his voice as he reached out to her. There was no way she was going to take his hand, much less get back in bed with him. She needed to keep as much distance as possible.

"No. I've got to get back and try to sneak into my room. What do you think my parents will say when they find my room empty this morning!" She was nearly screaming at him and becoming frantic. It didn't seem to give him any sense of urgency.

"Just text them that you got up early and went to school." His response was reasonable, but it didn't fit with Samantha's need to get away. He stood up and Samantha realized he was still completely naked. She looked away as he pulled up his boxers, her revelation about her feelings suddenly making her bashful.

That isn't going to work. I've got to go." She brushed past him heading toward the door. He grabbed her wrist and pulled her back against him. Her entire body stiffened. If he noticed, he didn't show it.

"I'll talk to you later," he said with a soft, sweet kiss before he let her go.

Samantha didn't respond. She had no intention of ever talking to Connor Grayson again!

CHAPTER TWELVE

The Loss

Eleven years ago...

Samantha practically ran the entire way home. She told herself it was to get home before her parents woke up, but in reality, it was because the burning in her lungs helped distract her from the ache in her chest. How could she have been so stupid? She set up rules to keep her distance from Connor, to keep her from breaking her heart. She had gone and broken her own rules and now she was in love with Connor Grayson. There was no denying it. She felt it every time she pictured his face. Was there any chance he could love her back? He called her his. He said he was hers. She felt their connection every time they were together. And he made love to her. Was it so hard to think that maybe they could have something real? That maybe he could love her?

He doesn't love you. You were a summer fling. He

is leaving for UCLA in a few weeks.

The voice was louder than the drumming of Samantha's pounding heart as she ran at full sprint back home. Samantha opened the back door to see her father sitting at the kitchen island in his pajamas, reading the paper. Her eyes went wide, her mouth dropped open, and she froze in the doorway. He lifted his coffee cup to his lips and took a slow sip, keeping his eyes on Samantha, silently demanding an explanation.

"Morning, Dad. You're up early. I was just going to head to school, but I forgot my bag." She tried to keep her voice calm as she lied to her Dad for the first time in as long as she could remember. She knew he could see right through her. Even if she wasn't covered in sweat and still panting from running away from Connor, she had always been a horrible liar. Her only hope was that her Dad didn't bother to challenge the obvious lie that sat between them, a giant elephant in the room.

"Mmmm, is that so?" he tested her. His look said, "is that really the story you want to go with?"

"I'm just going to grab my stuff and get going." Samantha tried to casually brush past him, hoping if she didn't acknowledge the lie, she could avoid the confrontation.

"Sammie, come sit with me for a second." He patted the seat next to him at the counter.

"I'm really running late, Dad…"

"Samantha, sit down." Using her full name was a red flag. He never called her Samantha. "I have been up for an hour. I know you were out all night. Let's stop pretending otherwise." The look on his face kept her from trying to object. He was right after all. She flushed with shame. She was caught. What must he think of her?

"When I first realized you weren't in your bed, I was terrified. I just about called the police." It killed her to think of the worry she caused him. She squirmed in her seat with the growing guilt in her heart. "Then, when I realized your wallet and cell phone were gone, it occurred to me you must have snuck out of the house, and I was furious

Samantha cringed. The thought of disappointing her dad was torture.

"I spent the better part of an hour devising new cruel and unusual forms of punishment while debating nailing your window shut." He said the words with almost a snort. It sounded strange and out of place. "You know what I realized then, Sammie?"

"What?" She was terrified of the answer. She braced herself to hear how disappointed he must be in her.

"I realized you are almost eighteen. You are basically an adult." The words caught Samantha off guard. Her eighteenth birthday was just a few weeks away, but she didn't really think of herself as an adult. It seemed like she was still screwing everything up too much to be considered anything other than a stupid kid.

"I may not like it, but my baby girl is growing up. You have always been responsible. Even when you were little, you refused to let us start the car until everyone had their seat belts on." He chuckled a bit at the memory. "Now you are a bright, beautiful, strong, and confident woman. I can't control what you do or the person you will become. Before long you are going to be at Stanford, making all kinds of decisions and choices about how you want to live your life. About the kind of person you want to be. I know you will make good choices. You always have. I trust you."

Tears began to stream down Samantha's cheeks at her father's words. When she most expected his censure, he was giving her his unconditional love. He believed in her and it made her believe in herself.

"I only ask two things of you, okay? First, promise me you will be safe. And, please don't lie to me again. Deal?"

"Deal." She barely got the words out before she reached out and hugged her father, basking in his acceptance and love. No one ever believed in her the way her father did.

"Okay. Now get to school. You are going to be late," they both laughed as they broke the soft moment.

"I can honestly say that last night was an accident." She wouldn't call being with Connor a mistake, but she hadn't meant to sleepover. Or, fall in love. "It is not likely to happen again anytime soon." She wasn't telling the whole story, but it was the truth. Her father accepted it and smiled as she made her way to her room.

"Oh, and let's not tell your Mom. I don't think she is ready to let go of you just yet. You'd still be wearing pigtails and getting walked to school if it were up to her! Love ya, Sammie," were his final words to her as she walked out of the kitchen.

Samantha was already hopelessly late, so she decided to go ahead and take a shower and change. There was a part of her that hated the idea of washing off Connor's scent, not being sure when or if she was ever going to see him again. In the end, her reason overtook her sentimentality. What was she going to do, never shower again?

As the warm water rushed down her body, she started to feel more confident. The conversation with her father had reminded her that she was a strong and capable woman. She wasn't nearly as terrified about being rejected by Connor. As she replayed the last few nights they had together, she began to let herself wonder for the first time if Connor Grayson could be in love with her.

Two nights ago after his baseball game he was so sweet and vulnerable. Last night, he held her in his arms. That morning, he reached for her as she was getting dressed. He wanted her to come back to bed with him. Even as she was leaving, literally running away from him, he grabbed her to give her a goodbye kiss and promised to talk to her soon. That didn't sound like someone who was desperate to get away from her. Samantha floated through most of the day in a dream awash with new possibilities. Possibilities for her and Connor to be together, really together. By the end of the day, those dreams would seem like a distant memory as her entire world came crashing down around her.

Elsie: I need you. Please come over.

Connor's phone lit up around seven. He was hoping to hear from Samantha today. She ran out of his room that morning like it was on fire. He was terrified she regretted being with him. As much as he wanted to hear from her, he had a bad feeling about this message. It was so much earlier in the day than any of their usual messages. It didn't feel right. Then she used the word need. Samantha never said she needed him. She didn't even say she wanted him. Her messages were always orders. Come over tonight. Be here by one. Now she was saying please. He was worried. Usually he walked so that no one saw his car parked outside her house, another one of Samantha's rules, but there was a feeling in the pit of his stomach that made him desperate to get to Samantha as quickly as possible.

He saw her as soon as he rounded the pathway to their backyard. She was sitting on the back step, her knees in her chest, her head buried in her arms. She looked broken. He started jogging to her, the need to take her into his arms nearly overwhelming.

"Samantha? Are you okay? What's wrong?" She lifted her head as soon as she heard his voice. Connor's eyes met hers and he could tell she had been crying. Not softly weeping, but soul shattering wailing. She jumped up and ran into his arms, nearly knocking him over with the force. He pulled her into him, holding her as tightly as he could, his body saying he would never let anything hurt her.

"He's gone. Connor, he's gone." Her voice was a soft whimper in his ear. He could barely hear it.

"Who? Who is gone?" He was trying to understand.

"My dad. There was an accident. He's gone." She collapsed into him entirely, sobbing uncontrollably. He swept her up into his arms and carried her to bed. He didn't care about walking into her house or being seen carrying her into her bedroom. All he carried about was taking care of her.

Still holding Samantha, Connor kicked off his

shoes and climbed onto her bed, cradling her to his chest. He sat back against the pillows, settling her into his lap, as he stroked her hair and kissed her forehead. He didn't say anything. He just held her until her sobs slowly quieted and started to subside.

"He was driving home from work. There was a truck that jack-knifed. He is dead." The words came out in little suffocated jerks, as if they were physically painful to say.

"I am so sorry." There wasn't more he could say. He didn't have the words to make her feel better.

"I can't believe he is gone. He was here this morning. Everything was fine this morning."

Connor continued to rub her back gently in the silence.

"You know he caught me? Sneaking in."

"Really? What did he say?"

"He said he trusts me and he loves me." Soft cries started to shake her body again. She grabbed fistfuls of Connor's shirt and buried her tearstained face in them.

"I'm sure he did. I am sure he loved you so much." Connor's words were both soothing and excruciating. Her father loved her very much, but she was never going to feel that love again. A silence passed between them once more. Connor didn't push. He was just there for her. Several hours went by with him holding her, crying intermittently with the occasional soft whisper of "I can't believe he is gone."

"I need to check on my Mom," were Samantha's first words after the several hours of silence. She pushed herself off his chest and let herself look at his face for the first time. He looked devastated, like her pain was his too. There wasn't any sense of pity, only compassion and commiseration.

"Do you want me to come with you?" His eyes were full of such loving tenderness.

"No, I need to go on my own," she kissed him softly on the lips as he brushed the most recent tears off her cheeks. Her kiss was a silent thank you. His touch said you are welcome.

While Samantha went to check on her mother, Connor made his way to the kitchen. He was rummaging through the refrigerator when she came back a few minutes later.

"She is still asleep," Samantha told him, taking in the scene before her. Connor was making a sandwich.

"Still?" Connor assumed Samantha's mother was asleep when he first arrived at least three or four hours ago.

"Yeah, the doctors at the hospital gave her some sort of sedative. She completely lost it there for a little while." Samantha shook with the memories of her mother's break down. She tried to push them aside. "What are you doing?" she asked Connor, bringing herself back to the here and now.

You should try to eat. I know you don't think you are hungry, but you should try." He wanted to take care of her. If her heart weren't broken it would be glowing. She walked around the counter and folded herself into his chest again. He wrapped her up in his big arms, making her feel safe under the weight of him. The sight of her mother came back to her, haunting images of her shattered family.

"She just completely broke down. It destroyed her. He is the love of her life. I have never seen her like that. I don't know how we are going to get through this." She spoke more to the world in general than to Connor.

"It will hurt and it will be hard, but you will make it through."

She didn't believe him, but it helped that he said them all the same.

"You didn't see her. She was hysterical. She just kept screaming and crying. They had to sedate her and I had to drive her home. She has been asleep ever since. I'm afraid she won't remember when she wakes up and I will have to tell her again that her husband is dead. How am I supposed to do that?"

"I don't know." His honest answer hung in the air as they clung to each other. After several minutes he kissed her head and spun her around slowly to face the sandwich on the counter. He kept his arms wrapped around her waist and his body pressed against hers. The warmth gave her comfort.

"Try to eat. Please, just a little. For me." His gentle words made her want to comply. She took a bite of the sandwich even though the thought of eating made her feel sick. She didn't taste anything. She took a small bite, chewed for what seemed like the right amount of time, and tried to swallow without gagging. She repeated these steps three times before the exhausting process was too much and she couldn't eat any more

"Drink this," Connor said as he pushed a glass of orange juice in front of her. Suddenly, thoughts of weekend breakfasts with her father popped into her head. It was his orange juice. He loved it. No one else drank it. This was the last bottle of orange juice her father would ever buy. Waves of grief rattled through her body. She thought of all the unknown lasts she had with her father. The last meal. The last talk. The last hug.

She collapsed back into Connor again, sobbing. He lifted her up and took her back to her room. He cradled her in his arms while she cried for the rest of the night. She fell asleep on his chest, her fists full of his shirt as if to make sure he didn't disappear as she slept. He made the worst night of her life bearable.

Rays of sun woke Samantha up the next morning, her first morning without her father. Connor was asleep underneath her, arms still tightly wrapped around her. She let her hands trace the line of his jaw and across his lips. Those familiar words floated in her head. I love you. She loved Connor Grayson and after last night she knew he loved her too. It would have been so easy to become dependent on that love, to need him. She felt it pulling her in even now as she watched his soft rhythmic breathing.

Her thoughts drifted to the image of her mother in the emergency room. She had completely shut down. The sight of her mother utterly broken terrified Samantha. Before she was a functioning human being. After, she was just a shattered shell of what used to be a woman. Samantha had been worried about the heartbreak if Connor didn't love her. She now knew the pain of rejection would be nothing compared to the crippling loss of his love after she had come to depend on it. Like her mother, she would crumble to dust, incapable of surviving a life without him.

As she looked down at the sleeping face of her first love, she remembered her last conversation with her father. You are going to be making decisions about how you want to live your life. About the kind of person you want to be. I know you will make good choices. She needed to be strong. She had to take care of her mother. She couldn't ever let herself breakdown. She couldn't ever let herself need anyone. She couldn't be with Connor. She loved him too much to survive losing him. A tear rolled town Samantha's cheek as she woke Connor up with a kiss. It was just one of a million tears she shed in the last twenty-four hours, but it was the first that wasn't for her father. This tear was for Connor and the final shattering of what was left of her tattered heart

"Connor, it's time to get up." Her voice was soft, but firm. She was beginning to regain some of the strength she lost yesterday. A new resolve dawned with the new day.

"Mmm, what time is it?" His voice was thick with sleep. Samantha tried to memorize the sound of it so she could treasure it later.

"It is almost eight. You are going to be late for practice."

"I can skip it today. I'm going to stay here and help you out." He sat up and tried to pull her towards him, but she was already out of his reach.

"No, it's okay. Really. I think I need to be alone with my mom today." She tried to hide the conflict in her voice. She desperately wanted him to stay, to help her, to be her strength, but she needed to stand on her own two feet. She needed to be able to get through this without him, without anyone.

"Okay, I get that," he said finally after looking her over, as if examining her for visible wounds to match the pain in her heart. It was clear he wanted to be there for her more than anything, but he didn't want to push. "Will you call me if you need anything?" He started following her to the backdoor, knowing by her body language she was saying goodbye.

"Sure," she answered, already knowing she wouldn't. He paused in the doorway, wrapping her in his arms one last time, pressing his forehead to hers.

"I love you," he said so softly she almost didn't hear. He said it because he wanted to. He had wanted to since almost the first second he saw her. And because he thought she needed to hear it.

"Thank you," was the only response she could give him. The three words she could never say choked her as she kissed him goodbye. She put her hand on his chest and pushed almost imperceptibly until he turned and walked away.

"I love you too," Samantha said to the closed door only after she was sure he was gone.

Samantha let several hours go by, trying to busy herself around the house and avoid thinking about the reality that had become her life now. She took her mother some food, trying to force her to eat as Connor had done for her last night. She did laundry. She took out the trash. She vacuumed the carpet. She mopped the floor. When the house was completely spotless and she ran out of chores, she let her mind drift to the things that needed to happen, the things her mother should be doing. She called her debate teacher and quit the team. She called her mom's work.

It took her awhile to figure out the right words to use. Simply saying there was a death in the family seemed belittling. That's what you say when a great aunt no one likes finally dies at the age of a hundred. Outright telling people her dad died in a car accident seemed too personal. She decided telling people she her father had passed was the compromise. She hated the word "lost" as if they could find him if they searched hard enough. Saying he had passed away made people think it wasn't as sudden, that they had time to adjust. It was mercifully vague enough that people made placid apologies and offered theoretical support.

Even with the right words, each conversation was excruciating. She could feel the awkward sympathy through the phone line and tried to harden herself to the pitying comments. Her parents were both only children with deceased parents, so the notifications were minimal, but so was the support. With her mom still incapacitated, Samantha was on her own. She spent the rest of her morning learning how to plan a funeral.

After she began at least enough planning to wait for her mother's decisions on location and pricing for the services, she turned her thoughts to Connor. She again tried to harden herself, this time to the idea of life without Connor. When she was sure Connor was in the middle of practice and wouldn't be looking at his phone, she sent him the message that she would regret nearly every day for the rest of her life.

Elsie: I can't do this anymore. I'm sorry. Thank you for everything. Please don't contact me again.

CHAPTER THIRTEEN

The Carving

Eleven years ago...

Connor hated walking away from Samantha that morning. She seemed so fragile last night and all he wanted to do was protect her. The memory of her tears tore his heart apart. He knew he couldn't do anything to make her pain go away, but at least when she was in his arms, he felt like he could prevent anything else from hurting her. But that wasn't what she wanted. She literally pushed him out the door this morning. She shut down. Connor was trying not to take her coldness personally. He was trying to respect the distance she seemed to need. It hurt that she barely even acknowledged him when he said he loved her, but he knew he was being selfish. Everything had to be about what she needed right now.

Connor drove back to his house after he left Samantha's. His parents hadn't noticed he was gone all night. Despite having barely slept and having a stiff back from leaning against Samantha's headboard for hours, Connor grabbed his bag and headed out to practice. Samantha asked to have the day to herself to deal with her mom. He knew he was going to need the distraction to keep from going back to her.

Connor was useless at practice. He was completely incapable of focusing. Just like the week after their first meeting, he couldn't keep himself from thinking about Samantha. Except now the thoughts weren't about touching her. They were about taking care of her. He was desperate to know how she was doing, what she needed, how he could help. He kept his phone on him all morning during warm-ups, checking it compulsively, until his coach had literally ripped it from his hand. He was banished to running laps for the remainder of practice. He ached to hear from Samantha. When the coach finally gave him back his phone after practice and he saw a missed message from her he kicked himself for not staying home. When he read the message, the physical pain was so severe, he dropped to his knees unable to breathe. It felt as if someone ripped his heart out of his chest.

Elsie: I can't do this anymore. I'm sorry. Thank you for everything. Please don't contact me again.

When he was finally able to draw a breath again, Connor exercised every ounce of willpower in his body not to call her back immediately. He didn't understand. He couldn't figure out why she pushed him away. Had he done something wrong? Was he not what she needed? He wanted to be so badly. Connor walked to his car in a confused haze. He sat in the parking lot staring out through his windshield, a million memories of his time with Samantha racing through his mind. When he started his car, he thought he didn't know where he was going. If he were honest, he knew there was only one place he could go. He drove to Samantha's.

Connor sat in his car outside of Samantha's house for two hours. He spent his time alternating between typing and deleting texts to her and searching the windows for glimpses of her. He even got out of the car once, took three steps toward her front door, and then turned back. He was torn between wanting to be there for her and wanting to honor her wishes for space. He was desperate to know why she suddenly needed space from him. Yesterday he was the one she needed. Today she didn't want him. Not knowing why was killing him.

After the third hour of his vigil, Connor drove home without seeing or hearing from Samantha. He locked himself in his room after a quick shower and grabbing a bite in the kitchen. He was exhausted yet restless. The exhaustion finally won out around one in the morning and he drifted off to sleep.

When his alarm went off five hours later, he felt like he had been hit by a bus. The first thing he did was grab his phone. Still no messages from Samantha. He let out a long sigh, dragging his hands down his face. He resolved to try his best to do what she asked, not to contact her. If he was honest, all the excuses he racked his brain yesterday to come up with for reaching out to here were selfish. She was hurting and this was what she asked from him. The least he could do was to give it to her despite how much as it killed him.

Connor spent the next two months keeping himself as busy as possible. He added another workout to his daily routine. He spent an extra hour at the batting cages. He researched the UCLA campus and started looking at classes. He spent time with his family. He started packing. He did everything he could to keep from thinking about Samantha. None of it worked. He walked by her debate classroom every day, even though he was pretty sure she dropped the class. He drove by her house at least once a day, although now he refused to let himself park outside. The only time he saw Samantha at all was weeks ago at her father's funeral. His family, as well as nearly everyone from the neighborhood, went to pay their respects. It was a short but personal service.

Samantha looked shaken, but strong. Her mom still seemed absent, like she was sleepwalking. Connor didn't know if that was because she was in shock or because she was still sedated. Samantha seemed to be the one in control. There were people constantly hovering around her, but she seemed so alone. From what Connor could tell, they didn't have any other family at the service. His heart ached for her. Ached to be with her. He watched her the entire service but made sure he stayed out of her line of sight. It wasn't until they were leaving the church that she saw him. Her mom's eyes were locked on the floor as if walking a tightrope, afraid to fall off. She clung to Samantha's arm like it was her only lifeline. Samantha's head was held high and she gave people silent little nods as they walked up the aisle behind the casket as if to say thank you for attending. When her eyes met Connor's, there was a brief second of recognition. He thought he saw a flash of longing in them before she looked away and continued with her little nods to the rest of the crowd. That look was all he had from her for two months.

It was the morning Connor was leaving for UCLA. He said his goodbyes to his family and friends. His car was packed and he was ready to hit the freeway. Instead, he found himself parked in front of Samantha's house. He knew he wasn't going to knock on her door. He wasn't expecting to see her. He just wanted to feel closer to her before he left, before they were done forever. He hoped that she would eventually reach out to him. When things settled down in her life, when her mother came back to her senses, he was sure she would come back to him. At the very least she owed him a real goodbye. He never got one. With one last sigh and a heavy heart Connor drove away, never expecting to see Samantha again.

Samantha knew that Connor was at UCLA, but her first day back at school she couldn't help herself from looking for him in every face she passed. She was desperate to see him over the past few weeks. She refused to call him, but every day she secretly hoped he would knock on her door. She missed him desperately. She knew she would give in if he reached out to her. He never did.

She avoided using their bathroom for the first month of her senior year even though it was the closest to her classes. She was afraid of the memories it would spark. Once she became accustomed to not seeing him, she forced herself to go inside of it. It was just a damn bathroom after all. As she reached out for the door handle to leave, she saw it, a carving of a four-leaf clover. It was well done for bathroom graffiti. Someone had taken their time. It was carved deeply into the wooden door, giving the leaves a sense of depth. She leaned in closer to see the writing around it.

Lucky loves Elsie forever

It was Connor. He must have carved it before he left, using their nicknames for each other as a final secret goodbye. Samantha bit into the side of her cheek, tasting blood as tears threatened to spring out of her eyes. She ran from the bathroom, trying to escape the memories of her first love. She didn't use that bathroom again for the rest of her senior year.

CHAPTER FOURTEEN

Monday Morning

They had only been apart a few days, but Samantha had spent every waking minute thinking of Connor. She saw him from across the office on Monday morning. He smiled the same easy smile at her, acting as if nothing had changed. His body language gave nothing away. He wore a soft pink dress shirt, the exact shade of the blush it caused on Samantha's cheeks. She chased away the butterflies dancing in her stomach with a swig of coffee and tried to focus on her work for the day.

Samantha knew the first order of business had to be clearing things up with Jessica. She was in the wrong for snapping at her last week. Connor's admonishment made sure Samantha knew it. The longer she put it off, the more embarrassing the mea culpa would be. Still, Samantha wasn't in a hurry to start her week off groveling. She wasn't good at apologizing, probably because she rarely did it. Admitting she was wrong was admitting weakness. If there was something Samantha hated more than anything else in the world, it was showing weakness.

The apology would have been easier if she felt more comfortable with where she stood with Connor. At least then she could have the last laugh, snatch victory out of the defeat knowing she was walking away with the prize Jessica sought with all her flirting. Samantha tried not to read into the fact she considered Connor to be the prize, one she might be tempted to win.

Her first date with Connor was awkward and confusing. The normal social pleasantries Samantha easily managed at many business dinners hadn't seemed appropriate with Connor. The simple act of making small talk was excruciating. The air around them felt charged, her words the spark. She was terrified to burn them both to ash. The result was frequent uncomfortable silences. A wave of jealousy flooded Samantha when she thought of how easily Connor and Jessica flirted. Why was it so hard for her? She knew how to flirt. She didn't date, but she knew how to attract a man when it suited her. She could bat her eyes and pucker her lips with the best of them. For some reason, she couldn't use those tricks with Connor. Samantha shook off her insecurities, calling Tammy into her office.

"Tammy, can you have Jessica come see me please?" If she was going to apologize, it was at least going to be on her terms. Everything with Samantha was a power play. Jessica knocked on Samantha's open door tenuously.

"Jessica, please come in and have a seat,"

Samantha said with a forced smile. Jessica took the seat she was directed to. She looked both irritated and intimidated. Being called into Samantha's office was rarely an enjoyable experience. There was a reason she had a reputation for being the office enforcer. She had impossible standards and was free with her critiques when someone failed to meet them. Jessica got a dose of that last week and wasn't excited for round two. Still, when Samantha Cane calls you to her office, you show up, take notes, and keep your mouth shut.

"I wanted to clear the air between us quickly this morning," Samantha started off neutral, trying to disarm Jessica a bit while easing herself into the distastefulness of apologizing. "Last week I was very direct with my critique of your work. If I was short with you, or I didn't provide you the necessary direction, I want to apologize. Perhaps my comments would have been more appropriate in a private setting." Samantha crammed enough conditional statements into her apology to avoid any actual culpability. Saying she wanted to apologize wasn't actually apologizing. Still, Jessica seemed placated sufficiently judging by her satisfied smirk. That smirk was a mistake. Now Samantha was irritated. Her mind flashed back to Jessica's hand on Connor's arm the previous week and she snapped.

"As I am sure you are aware, this is a very important time for this team and I need to ensure we are all focused and contributing." Not flirting like a dog in heat with the hired consultant. The unsaid implication wafted in the air between them. Jessica shifted in her seat uncomfortably, not meeting Samantha's eyes. Samantha was pleased at the thought that even if Connor wanted to flirt with Jessica, she wouldn't reciprocate. Jessica was more afraid of Samantha than she was attracted to Connor. A victory was a victory, even if she had to imply threats to get it.

"I understand. I am committed to this team and this merger," was Jessica's timid response.

"Great! I'm so glad to hear it. And, I am glad we had this chat. I look forward to seeing the improvement in your work this week." Jessica's eyes flared at Samantha's words. She wanted to argue, but one look from Samantha kept her silent. She shuffled out of Samantha's office biting on her lip to keep back the retort she desperately wanted to throw at Samantha. Turning her eyes back to her screen with satisfaction, Samantha continued with her Monday morning routine when she heard the familiar husky voice from her office door.

"You are the queen of passive aggressiveness!" Connor said with a chuckle as he flopped into a chair in front of her, making himself at home. It hadn't escaped Samantha's notice that he didn't knock. Her eyes snapped back to her office door where Tammy was hovering, her eyes pleading forgiveness for allowing the intrusion. Some gatekeeper Timid Tammy ended up being. One look at Connor's smug face was all it took for Samantha to know been eavesdropped on her chat with Jessica, too intrigued by it to interrupt earlier.

"Is there something I can help you with this morning, Connor?" She kept her tone cold and detached, making sure he knew she didn't appreciate his familiarity.

"There is something I can help you with." He

paused just long enough to pique her interest. Her thoughts turned naughty faster than she wanted to admit. Connor's smirk told her he knew exactly the thoughts she was having. "You know you are not well liked in this office? And with conversations like that I'm not surprised."

"I don't much care for being liked. I am respected," was her curt response.

"No. You are feared which isn't doing our team any favors."

Our team? Samantha cringed at the realization Connor was trying to include her on his team when she was only been concerned with being at the top of the pyramid. She tried to ignore his words, but they rang true. She had power, but she wasn't part of the team. She remembered the meeting where he brought everyone together, engaged with everyone and getting them excited about the merger. That wasn't a skill she had. "Doesn't play well with others" was going to be carved into her tombstone.

I can help you with that. Smooth over some of those rough edges of yours," his voice wasn't placating or condescending. It was sincere and sweet. Still, Samantha wasn't ready to admit she was wrong. Never admit weakness.

"Who I am has gotten me where I am today. I think I am doing just fine, thank you." Samantha was trying hard to believe it. She wanted to be enough on her own. She needed to be.

"Fair enough. My services are here if you change your mind." His voice had taken a vaguely sexy tone with the innuendo. "Now, on to what I actually came here for. It seems like your poor assistant is afraid to schedule any meetings now without your explicit say-so. She must respect you too much," he said with a smirk and a wink.

"What meeting would you like to schedule?" She ignored his teasing.

"We have a video teleconference with Hiro today at three."

"Hero?"

"Hirotami Kojima, the principal at Keiretsu Holdings."

"Oh, Hiro," Samantha said sheepishly trying to hide her embarrassment. She was so busy handling her side of the merger that she hadn't been involved at all with Keiretsu Holdings. "I wasn't aware he wanted to have a meeting. Isn't it a bit early in the process for that?"

"We've exchanged a bunch of e-mails back and forth now and I think it is the perfect time to put a face to a name. We aren't looking to make any actual policy decisions. Mainly, we are just going to be setting the agenda for our trip to Tokyo next week."

"Excuse me? Our what?" Samantha was in shock. She had no idea she was supposed to be going to Tokyo. She assumed Mr. Slone would be doing all the senior executive engagements. Why was Connor always one step ahead of her? It drove her crazy.

"I talked to Slone about it this weekend at lunch."

Of course Connor was having lunch with her boss over the weekend. They were best friends now!

"He isn't keen to leave Abby for an entire week. Plus, he said he has complete confidence in your abilities," Connor said with his flirty voice again.

"Abby?" Samantha was reeling this morning from all the information she didn't have.

"Abigail Slone, his wife." Connor's networking

skills were on a whole new level. Samantha couldn't keep her eyes from rolling. If she were honest to herself, she was a little jealous. She wasn't a people person and she knew it hurt her career

She was sure Mr. Slone's confidence in her was largely based on Connor's endorsement. While she was extremely appreciative of the opportunity Connor laid at her feet with this trip, she was also extremely annoyed that it wasn't based on her actual accomplishments. She worked hard. To be gifted this trip based on Connor's sweet talking was insulting. She had shown enough dedication and competency over the past several years to earn this trip entirely on her own merit. What was that saying about gift horses?

"You do have a passport, right?" Conner pulled Samantha out of her irritation and self-consciousness.

"Of course I have a passport!" Her indignation was potent. She had a passport. It had never been used, but she knew it existed somewhere in her apartment. She really hoped it wasn't expired.

"Great." Connor ignored her hostility. He was good at that, treating her like she wasn't abrasive. "So, video teleconference at three, and we'll finalize our travel details on Wednesday night."

"Wednesday night?" Samantha felt like she had been behind the curve this entire conversation. Connor had that effect on her. She was never really in control of herself when he was around.

"I am taking you to an art gallery opening. Pick you up at seven." It was a statement, not a question. Samantha had no vote in the matter. After taking a moment to revel in the confusion in her eyes, Connor got up and strutted out of her office.

Samantha watched the sexy figure of Connor Grayson leaving her office in his pink shirt with a smile she couldn't prevent. He was the only person who made her feel out of control in a way that both excited and infuriated her. He was brazen and confident. He was everything she wasn't. She craved to have more of him even as her mind screamed danger warnings between her ears.

CHAPTER FIFTEEN

The Second Date

The video teleconference went smoothly, largely due to Connor's charm. Samantha was amazed at how he seemed to have an instant report with Hiro based simply on an e-mail conversation. How did he do that? How did he make everyone feel like they were the most interesting person in the world? Maybe she could learn a few things from him, not that she'd ever tell him that.

By Wednesday, Samantha was almost used to seeing Connor at work. She was still hyper-aware of every moment they were alone together, but he was exceptionally professional. He wasn't any more affectionate or familiar with Samantha than he was with any other member of the team. Samantha told herself she was appreciative and thought they were on track to stay work colleagues. In reality, she was irritated he didn't flirt with her. Mercifully, he didn't flirt with anyone else either. Samantha was jealous of pretty much anyone else who held Connor's attention for longer than five minutes, but he was sensitive of not give special attention to anyone, much to Jessica's disappointment.

Samantha was too busy overanalyzing their interactions to get much work done. Wednesday night came quicker than she thought it could. Despite the trepidation, Samantha was looking forward to seeing Connor out of work again. Thoughts of their kiss still caused her to flush, but she refused to admit they could be anything other than co-workers who happened to have a past.

The decision on what to wear this time was quicker for Samantha. She wore a trendy dark blue lace dress with a full skirt hitting her high on the thigh, sheer on the arms and low cut on the back. It reeked of sex. She rationalized the outfit to herself by claiming it was the only thing she owned hip enough to wear to an art gallery opening. Samantha would never admit, but she constantly wore dresses around Connor to increase the chances of feeling his hands against her naked thighs.

Connor was prompt at seven. This time Samantha was waiting for him on the curb, avoiding the awkward text. Something told her he still didn't trust her enough to be alone in her apartment. Smart man.

"You look amazing." Connor's voice dripped with desire, causing Samantha's lips to curl into a smile at the small victory.

"So do you." she wasn't lying. Connor was in another bespoke suit with a crisp white button-down shirt. Unlike work, he wasn't wearing a tie. Instead the top two buttons of his shirt were undone, letting just the hint of his masculine chest to peek out. Samantha's mouth watered at the sight of the extra bit of his tan skin. She couldn't help but wonder if his body was still as toned and luxurious as the last time, she ran her hands along it. Without realizing it, she was biting her bottom lip at the memory. The sight made Connor chuckle knowingly. The same memories flooded his mind after seeing her long legs and bare back in that dress. He squirmed uncomfortably in his seat, his pants suddenly tighter than before.

They drove silently to the art gallery, unspoken desires and lust thick in the air as they drove. Connor thought long and hard about what to do on a second date with Samantha. Their first date was less than great. An intimate dinner was too much for two people with so much they were trying not to say to each other. He thought about taking her to a movie or a play, but that seemed like a waste of time. Why bother going on a date when you spend the entire time not talking to each other? Plus, too long with Samantha under the cover of darkness could lead them down a dangerous path. He wanted to be with her, but he needed it to be more than sex. This time, he wanted all of her.

For their second date, he needed something with more distraction than dinner but more engaging than a play. When he received the invite to this art gallery opening it seemed like the perfect option. Now that they were here, wandering around the gallery it seemed as awkward as their first date. Neither were art experts and he struggled to find something to say to her about any of the pieces. He was never this self-conscious around women. But Samantha wasn't just any woman. She was the one that got away, the one he still wanted. They ended up hovering around each other, not talking, like planets trapped orbiting each other without ever getting closer. After half an hour they were both noticeably frustrated by the awkwardness. Connor was ready to push the boundaries to close the distance.

her back as she stood in front of an abstract painting, more stunned by the price than wowed by the art. The feel of his warm fingers on her back made her aware of every inch of skin on her body. She tingled from head to toe, trying to stifle the moan his simple touch was instigating in her throat. Nothing but work colleagues for sure.

"Is this your favorite?" The feeling of his steamy breath on her neck drove her crazy. She leaned back into him, intensifying the tingling across her body with the contact.

"I hate it actually," she said in a half whisper. She wasn't concerned about someone else hearing her. She wanted to hold onto the growing feeling of intimacy between them.

"And, why is that?" His voice was calm and even in her ear. Was he not as affected by their connection as she was? He had to be.

"If I'm going to pay the price of a new car for something to hang on my wall, it better be something nicer than I could do on my own with twenty bucks and a bottle of wine."

Connor chuckled at her words. The sound stirred something in her, something better than desire. The sound of his sweet laugh caused an ache in her chest. She longed to hear it again. She tried to push the feeling aside and focus on the lust she felt moments before.

"So, you are an artist now too? Is there anything you can't do Samantha?" There was a disarming tenderness in his words. Without thinking Samantha turned her eyes up to his. What she found there took her breath away. Like hers, they held lust and desire, but underneath there was something deeper. More pure. There was longing and devotion. It drew Samantha in against her will. She leaned in and pressed a soft kiss on his lips. They were both captured in a moment of pure tenderness as the rest of the world drifted away. Samantha pulled away first, like she always did. She didn't let her eyes meet his again. She didn't say a word. She just walked away, refusing to acknowledge the moment they shared.

Samantha was desperate to run away. She needed to put distance between herself and Connor, physically and emotionally. She was hoping with distance the longing that she saw in his eyes would fade. If she could get far enough away, the devotion she felt growing in her heart would wither. She had to find a way to push him away to protect them both. She couldn't give him what he wanted. She couldn't be what he wanted.

Samantha rounded the corner of the gallery and her eyes lit up at the sight of a handicapped bathroom. It was secluded in the corner of one of the shows. If she lingered by one of the sculptures, she was sure she could maneuver Connor into it before he realized what was happening. Suddenly, she knew how to kill the longing in Connor's eyes. She was going to drown it in lust and smother it with desire. After all, if their relationship was about sex, she could pretend it wasn't anything deeper.

AMELIA KINGSTON

She had her ambush set. She was still, staring at
the wire sculpture in front of her like a spider lying in
wait for her pray. Less than five minutes later,
Connor was next to her, placing his hand on the small
of her back again, dipping his fingers into the skin just
above her hips. Samantha closed her eyes to focus on
the sensation, warmth radiating from his hands across
her body. Snapping out of her reverie, she
remembered her plan. Make tonight about desire and
sex, not longing and devotion.

"There is something special I wanted to show
you." Her words were haughty. She tried to keep her
tone even as desire started to overtake her. She
wanted to have him in the only way she could. She
grabbed his hand and led him towards the bathroom.
As she got to the door, she turned around to face
him.

"How about it, Lucky? For old time's sake?" she
quipped with a sexy smirk, refusing to let go of his
hands. Samantha couldn't read his face. There was
certainly desire in his eyes. Samantha was familiar
enough with that. There was also a hint of something
else. Was it disappointment? Before Connor could
pull back, Samantha opened the door to the
bathroom and pulled him in. As soon as the door
closed, she pulled him to her. The awkwardness that
surrounded them most of the night melted away as
they both gave in to their passion.

One of Samantha's hands gripped a fist full of
Connor's shirt. The other, she dragged through his
hair, grabbing the back of his neck, and pulling him
down to her. Connor was resisting slightly as their lips
first pressed together. His body was stiff, his hands at
his sides. Samantha's kiss was a challenge. Touch me.

Be with me. She kissed him without him kissing back, pressing her body into his with wanton desire.

"Please kiss me." The plea left Samantha's lips before she could think about what it meant. She hadn't intended to beg him. She hoped to seduce him, make him a slave to his own desire. Instead, she was the one desperate for his touch. Her soft plea broke down Connor's last resistance. His hand reached up to her hips, pulling them against his, before sliding up her side, grazing her breast, brushing across her jaw and settling at the back of her neck curled in her hair.

"Fuck it," was his breathy reply before smashing his lips against hers. His kisses were hostile. His lips devoured her. He grabbed the outside of her thighs and lifted her up onto the sink, stepping between her legs. Samantha felt like her whole body was on fire. She wrapped her legs around his hips to keep him from pulling away. The wave of passion overtook them. Their hands roamed each other's bodies without restraint while their tongues explored each other's mouths. Samantha moaned in pleasure as she rocked her hips against his. She could feel his arousal growing between her legs. She wanted all of him.

"I want you. So bad." It was an admission Samantha hadn't been prepared to make. She wanted to force him to his knees in desire, make him admit their connection was physical. Instead, she lost herself in her need for him. Her hands found his belt buckle just before his fingers clasped down on top of them.

"Wait." He stopped her, pulling away with a deep sigh.

"What's wrong?" It felt like he dumped a gallon of ice water over her head. She shuddered. The few inches between them now an insurmountable chasm.

A sudden emptiness tore through Samantha's heart.

"I want more than." He sounded defeated. It broke her heart. He was staring down at her hands in his, unwilling to meet her eyes. She had a sudden urge to hug him, to hold him to her chest until he understood how much he meant to her. How much he would always mean to her. But, she couldn't. Images of her mother, devastated and destroyed, unwittingly flashed into her mind. She clung to the memory, letting the feelings of loss, terror, and emptiness kill the growing need inside her chest. She knew even if she could be with him now, that was how it would end. How it always had to end. Inevitably, love was pain.

"Why is this so easy—" Samantha gestured between them. "And that is so hard?" Samantha gestured out to the world waiting to suffocate them beyond the door. He knew what she was asking. Their bodies always fit together. It was natural, effortless. He knew how to touch her, but not how to talk to her. At least, not how to talk to her without her shutting down and pushing him away.

"Simple. This is safe." He gestured between them. "That scares you. That matters." He gestured to the door behind him as his eyes met hers. Samantha felt ashamed. Connor deserved so much more. He deserved someone who would give him everything, someone who wouldn't hold back. Samantha would never be able to give him what he wanted. She couldn't. She needed to be strong. She would always keep him at arm's length for her own survival.

"I'm sorry." She didn't know what else to say. She wanted to give him everything, but she couldn't let herself.

"I know." Connor didn't say more. He didn't need to. He kissed her on the forehead before leaving the bathroom. Samantha stayed locked away for another ten minutes, fighting back the tears she wanted to cry for Connor. For herself. For their discarded love.

She found Connor toward the gallery entrance waiting for her. They didn't speak. The silence wasn't awkward this time. Now it felt like a conclusion, the end of her and Connor. Samantha reached across the car and grabbed Connor's hand from off his knee. She didn't look at him. She didn't say a word. She merely interlocked her fingers with his and held tightly for the rest of their hushed drive. It was an acknowledgement of her want for things to be different. Together they silently mourned the death of their love.

When he pulled up to her house, neither spoke a word. There was no need. Samantha slid out of the passenger seat and walked up to her apartment. That night she cried harder than she had in eleven years. Her heart broke open again. When she was finally overcome by sleep, her pillow was soaked with eleven years of her regrets.

CHAPTER SIXTEEN

The Dance

On Thursday Connor didn't come to the Phillip, Morrissey & Tanner office. Instead, he worked from Republic Consulting for the first time since the merger began. The whole office felt his absence, but no one as much as Samantha. She hadn't realized how much she had grown to like working with him, watching him. She was lethargic, unmotivated for the first time in as long as she could remember. Every little thing she did felt exhausting, checking e-mails, answering the phone, sitting in meetings. All she wanted to do was crawl back into bed and pull the covers overhead. Somehow, she trudged through the rest of the day. Tammy wandered into her office around two in the afternoon, breaking up the monotony.

"I just received your travel itinerary from Brianna. It looks like you will be flying out on Sunday evening.

Would you like me to arrange for a town car to take you to the airport?" Samantha was too distracted to be annoyed at her lack of knocking.

"Who is Brianna?"

"Connor's assistant," Tammy responded easily, unaware of the knife she was twisting in Samantha's heart. Connor wouldn't even bother to e-mail her their itinerary himself. He had to have his assistant contact her assistant. He needed two degrees of separation from her. She shouldn't have been surprised, but she was still hurt.

"Don't bother with a town car. I'll just take a cab," Samantha's response was curt. She spent the rest of the afternoon trying and failing to avoid thinking about Connor. Around three she sent him an e-mail to confirm she received his literary and would meet him at the gate on Sunday unless he wanted to arrange transportation for them both. It was a completely professional e-mail that she could have sent Mr. Slone. There were no tricks, no innuendo, no references to their last two dates. Still, it meant something more than the words. It was a gesture. An olive branch. Connor didn't reply. After finally giving up on accomplishing anything remotely worthwhile, Samantha went home, crawled into bed, and wallowed.

On Friday, Connor was back. When Samantha heard his voice talking to Tammy outside of her office, she let out an audible sigh. It felt like she had been holding her breath for two days and was finally able to breathe again. In less than two weeks Connor somehow became part of her life. Not just her work, her life. Just having him near her both calmed and excited her, made her feel more complete in ways she didn't understand and would never admit. Samantha sat in her office chair, closed her eyes and listened to the sound of Connor's voice. He was too far away for her to make out what he was saying, but the melodic tones still eased the ache in her heart.

His voice started to trail off and Samantha followed it, getting up from her seat and walking towards the door. She couldn't resist the urge to stay close to Connor. Just as she reached her doorway, Tammy popped up in front of her, blocking the way.

"Oh sorry," Tammy said with a start. "I was just coming in to tell you Connor wanted to schedule a working dinner tonight

Samantha craned her head around Tammy looking for Connor. She made out the shape of his broad shoulders and muscular back as he walked away from her to the other side of the office. Her mind was willing him to turn around, to look back at her. He didn't.

Samantha's attention fell back to Tammy. Connor came to schedule a working dinner. Not a date. He didn't ask Samantha. He scheduled it through Tammy. They were just work colleagues now. Samantha never knew victory could taste so bitter.

"What time?"

"He said he would pick you up at your apartment at six thirty," Tammy read off her notes.

If Samantha hadn't been so distracted, she might have heard the sappy tone in Tammy's voice. Tammy obviously thought it was a date and expected Samantha to turn into some cliché cartoon character with stars in her eyes and her heart beating out of her chest. If only she was as sure as Tammy of her happy ending.

"Thank you, Tammy," Samantha said dismissively. Tammy walked back to her desk and sat down, obviously disappointed in the lack of butterflies in her boss' stomach. Samantha stood in her doorway, staring at the back of Connor Grayson, drinking in the sight of him knowing the time they had together was ticking away. After the merger, he would be out of her life again. She took the time to try and memorize every little detail about him, the color of his hair, the shape of his body, the softness of his lips, the sound of his laugh. Samantha clung to those images, locking them away deep in her heart.

"Did you need something else, Ms. Cane?" Tammy's voice made Samantha realize she was still standing awkwardly in her doorway staring at Connor. This time Samantha did notice the teasing smile on Tammy's lips at catching her boss ogling the office hottie.

"No, thank you. Please tell Connor that I am available tonight," Samantha said, blushing as she returned to her desk. She pulled out her phone and stared at Connor's name in her contacts. She typed out a message. Then, deleted it. Then, typed out a new one before deleting that one as well. She did that for fifteen minutes before slamming her phone down with a huff. She turned back to her work, trying to focus on anything but Connor Grayson. She managed it for all an hour before she picked up her phone again, hovering over his name. This time her fingers flew over the words and hit send before she could stop herself.

Samantha: What should I wear tonight?

Samantha stared at her phone, willing Connor to respond. Thirty minutes went by with nothing. Her foot was bouncing with tension as she chewed on her nails, eyes never leaving her screen. She slammed her phone down again, irritated with Connor and disappointed in herself. She turned her attention back to the financial reports on her computer. When her phone finally chimed, she nearly jumped out of her seat reaching for it.

Connor: Something conservative.

Samantha's heart sank. How much had changed in just a few days. For their first date he told her to wear something sexy. Now, he wanted her to dress conservative for their business dinner. The same feeling of exhaustion from yesterday was back. She had a million things she to get done before she left to Japan with Connor on Sunday, but she was struggling to focus. It took all her energy to finish the minimum tasks for the day. For the first time since she had started working at Phillips, Morrissey & Tanner, she left early. She told Tammy it was because she needed to pack and get ready for the trip. Really, she was too tired to keep working.

Samantha stripped off her shoes and crawled into bed when she got home. It was only just after four o'clock. She had two hours until Connor was picking her up. She couldn't think about that, about him. She pulled the covers over her head and wallowed.

Connor: I'm downstairs.

Samantha woke with a start. It wasn't until she got

the text from Connor that she realized she had fallen asleep. She wasn't anywhere near ready. She ran to the bathroom. Her mascara was smeared, she had pillow face, and a wicked case of bed hair. Very professional. Connor asked for conservative and was getting frumpy. Samantha quickly started to clean herself up as she texted Connor.

Samantha: Running late. Give me fifteen minutes.

She fixed her make-up, pulled back her hair into a messy chic bun low on her neck, and grabbed the first dress her hand landed on in the closet. Luckily, the dress worked. It was conservative, but still sexier than her normal work attire. It was a flowing emerald green wrap dress with a boat neck that exposed her tan shoulders without too much cleavage. Samantha rushed out the door, taking a quick glance at herself in the mirror as she went. The green brought out the flush on her cheeks from the frenzy of getting ready. She didn't look as polished as she usually did, but not bad for fifteen minutes post-nap. Good enough for a work dinner she thought with a sigh.

"Sorry I'm late," Samantha said as she jumped into his SUV. He was wearing the same suit from work. It was the first time he hadn't changed to meet her, one more reminder that she was just another colleague now. Samantha's heart dropped.

"Don't worry about it," Connor was curt, giving her a quick glance before driving off. They drove in complete silence for twenty minutes, tension thick in the air. Samantha racked her brain to think of something to say.

"Have you been to Japan before?" Small talk with

Connor felt weird, but it was better than silence.

"Several times," his response wasn't even a full sentence. He didn't look over at her. Why did he ask her to a work dinner if he was still this angry at her?

"Any recommendations for what I should pack? Anything special?" Samantha was trying to engage him in any way. His aloofness was torture.

"Make sure you bring an adaptor."

"Adaptor?"

"Power adaptor. They have different plugs."

"Right." Samantha felt stupid for not thinking of that. She had never left the country before, except for the senior trip to Mexico. Power adapters hadn't been at the top of her packing list at eighteen.

"We're here," Connor announced as he pulled into a dimly lit parking lot. Samantha tried to figure out where they were. It looked like some kind of school.

"I don't underst—"

"I lied. This isn't a business dinner." He cut her off. His voice was softer, having more a tone of guilt than annoyance, but he still refused to look at Samantha. "I made arrangements for us before…" his voice trailed off. She knew the words it hurt too much to say. Before I gave up on us. "Before Wednesday. And I couldn't really get out of them. I figured, screw it. I might as well bring you anyway. I lied because I didn't think you'd come otherwise." Samantha's heart fluttered in her chest. He hadn't given up on her, not yet.

"Okay." Samantha couldn't help the smile that crept onto her lips. "So, why are we at a school then?"

"It's my niece's first dance. I promised my sister I'd chaperone." Samantha's smile grew at the thought.

This wasn't just a date, he was including her in a part of his life, his family. "I was afraid when I told you to dress conservatively, you'd do the opposite just to spite me." Connor finally looked over at her, catching her gaze in his.

"I probably would have if I thought about it," Samantha chuckled. "You know me, I live to be difficult." She was trying to be playful, but she only got a quick half smile in return. Connor looked like a prisoner on death row. He wasn't dead yet, but he knew it was coming soon and he couldn't stop it. Samantha didn't want to be his executioner.

"Do you want to know a secret?" Samantha paused to see the shift on Connor's face from resignation to curiosity. Good, progress. "I was asleep when you texted. I'd crawled in bed after work and just passed out! That's why I was running late."

He looked at her, eyeing her up and down as if deciding if she was telling the truth.

"You're not sleeping well these days either?" They shared a silent acknowledgement of the reason for their mutual insomnia. "That explains why you look...less...put together." He was slow and deliberate with his word choice. A smirk was just peeking out on the corner of his lips.

"Hey!" Samantha shrieked in fake irritation as she reached across the car and smacked his arm. He laughed out loud, a full belly laugh. It was contagious. Samantha couldn't help but laugh with him. It was now a cycle, Samantha's laugh making Connor laugh harder, and his doing the same to her, until they were both laughing like escaped mental patients. They laughed until their stomachs ached and their eyes watered. And with that the tension was broken.

"I think you look beautiful," Connor confessed as their laughing eased. He reached across his car and tucked a loose strand of hair behind her ear. The intimacy made Samantha blush. Connor loved those rosy cheeks. "Let's go." He jumped out of the car to avoid leaning across and kissing her.

Connor took her hand as they walked into the junior high school gym. A wave of nostalgia swept Samantha at the sight of balloons, crape paper, and streamers. A cute brunette girl with Connor's lips came storming up to them.

"Uncle Connor! What. Are. You. Doing. Here!" The girl's tone thick with indignation.

"I'm here for the dance, just like you shortcakes," Connor replied with his normal easy charm.

"Urgh." She clearly didn't believe him. "I told Mom I didn't need a babysitter! I'm not a kid. You better not do anything to embarrass me!"

"Don't worry, I've got great moves." Connor busted out running man followed by the sprinkler.

"Oh my God! You are so ridiculous! I can't even!" She screeched as she stormed off, clearly not appreciating his classic dance style.

"Love you too, shortcakes," Connor called after her, making Samantha laugh. She knew he had three sisters, but never actually met any of them. It was sweet to think of him as goofy Uncle Connor.

"Come on, let's get some punch." Connor guided her to the snack table before they took a seat on the bleachers. Connor finally let go of Samantha's hand as they took their seats but sat close enough to her that their knees touched. That gentle tickle made Samantha crave more.

"Your niece seems like a firecracker."

"Yeah, she takes after Diane for sure. Always so bossy."

"Diane is your older sister?"

"Yep, the first of the four Graysons. Diane, Connor, Allison, and Katherine. Diane always thought she was the boss because she was the oldest. And baby Katie could get away with murder because she was the youngest and the cute blonde one. The rest of us look like Dad, but Katie looks just like my mom. Blonde hair, blue eyes, dimples. She was a terror!" Connor's eyes lit up with loving memories. His family meant a lot to him.

"And what about Allison?" Samantha asked, noticing he hadn't said anything about his middle sister. She wanted him to keep going, wanted to know more about him and what made him who he is.

"Allie was a tomboy. We were two peas in a pod, for a while at least."

"What happened?"

"She discovered make-up, and dresses. And boys. Eventually one of my best friends noticed her. They're getting married in the spring," he said with a mix of pride and sadness. Samantha couldn't place why.

"That is sweet," Samantha said it more to the air than to Connor. She watched young couples fill the dance floor as a slow song started to play over the speakers.

"Sickeningly sweet," Connor said with a smirk. Samantha turned back to face him, the familiar look of longing back in his eyes. It didn't scare Samantha as much this time. This time she bathed in it, feeling it well up inside of her heart.

Come dance with me," Samantha asked as she

stood up and held out her hand. He took it without hesitation and led her to the dance floor, wrapping his arms around her waist and pulling her into him.

Do you ever wonder what it would have been like?" he asked.

"What?" His words had interrupted her memorizing the feeling of being in his arms.

"Us. Back in high school. If we had been together," he paused as his voice got heavier. "Really together."

"It would've been great." Samantha answered honestly, moved his devotion-soaked words. Wrapped in his arms, she wondered what it would have been like to be Connor Grayson's girlfriend. It would've been amazing, until it wasn't. Until it ended. And it would always end one way or another. "For a while." The words hung in the air between them, thick with meaning. With Samantha's fear. Samantha pulled Connor closer, tucking herself into his chest, trying to hide from the pain she knew would come from letting go.

They stayed wrapped in each other's arms until a fast pop song began to fill the gym. They returned to their seat on the bleachers, but this time Connor didn't let go of Samantha's hand. Their fingers stayed intertwined in his lap for the rest of the dance. They didn't speak, there didn't seem to be anything else to say.

Connor dropped his niece and two of her friends off at Diane's before driving to Samantha's apartment. They didn't speak in the car ride, an excruciating change from the constant squealing and chattering that had come from the three twelve-year olds in the back seat. When he pulled up out front of her building, Samantha didn't get out. She sat there, looking up at her building, quietly thinking.

"Are you okay?" Connor asked her with a touch of concern beginning to overtake the sadness she knew he felt. She felt it too. She wasn't prepared for goodbye. She turned in her seat and looked directly in his eyes. Then she knew what she had to do.

"Will you come up for a minute?"

"Samantha..." he was shaking his head.

"Please Connor. I just want to show you something. It will be quick." Her voice was pleading, but still he didn't respond. He just stared into her while deciding. Samantha didn't breathe again until he unbuckled his seatbelt. Her heart did a flip. Her elation was short lived, being quickly replaced by overwhelming terror. But she wouldn't back down now. He deserved to see it. He deserved to know. That was the least she could do.

Connor followed Samantha into the building, keeping his distance, his hands never leaving his pockets. Samantha opened the door to her apartment and they both stepped inside without speaking. Samantha crossed the living room before she realized Connor wasn't following her. He wasn't budging from the doorway.

"It's in my bedroom."

"Go get it, I'll be here." He was defiant. That wasn't going to work. He needed to see it where it was.

"Please Connor. This is important," she urged.

"Samantha..." His body was tense. He said her name as a warning.

"I promise to keep my hands to myself." She held up her hands in surrender to show her innocent intentions. Letting out an edgy growl, he followed her into her bedroom.

"It's there." Samantha stepped aside just inside her bedroom and pointed up to a small framed picture over her bed. Connor took a few tentative steps into the room, unable to make out the picture. Samantha flipped on the light and Connor finally recognized it. It wasn't a picture. It was a rubbing. She had framed a rubbing of the carving he made her on their bathroom door half a lifetime ago. Connor leaned over the bed and took the frame off the wall, sitting down on the side of Samantha's bed, completely overwhelmed.

Lucky loves Elsie forever.

Connor was too distracted, tracing the lines of the rubbing, to notice Samantha crossed the room to stand in front of him. He didn't look up when she started speaking.

"It's been framed above my bed since the day I left for college. Everywhere I've lived, the first thing I did was hang it up. It is special to me." You are special to me. She couldn't bring herself to finish the confession. She didn't need to. This was enough. For a while.

"Come here." Connor's voice was husky and needy. It made Samantha's stomach flutter uncontrollably.

"I promised..." She reminded him. It didn't matter. Connor leaned forward and grabbed her hips, pulling her on top of him. Her knees were on either side of him, straddling his as he sat on the edge of the bed, just like their first time. Samantha dropped her forehead to meet Connor's as she wrapped her arms around his neck. They sat there, connected, letting the words go unspoken.

As they sat breathing each other in, Connor's hands slowly slid down her sides and pulled up the hem of her dress. Samantha's heart felt like it would beat out of her chest as she felt Connor lift the fabric up and over her head, before letting it fall to the floor. She unbuttoned his shirt, placing soft kisses lower and lower, letting her fingers take over when her lips could no longer reach. He reached around and unhooked her bra, letting it slowly fall off her shoulders, before pulling her into him, her bare chest to his. The warmth of his skin on hers made Samantha let out a soft moan. Connor picked her up, spun them around and gently placed her back on the bed before standing up. He stood at the edge of the bed, memorizing her body, naked except for her lace panties.

Samantha's body seemed to chill from the sudden distance, her nipples perking. She locked her eyes on his, searching for him in their silver depths. For a moment she thought Connor was going to grab his shirt off the floor and walk out. Then, he grabbed his belt buckle and dropped his slacks and boxers in a single motion. He reached down and slowly pulled off her panties, her skin tingling at his touch tracing over every inch of her legs. They each took a breath, taking a moment to appreciate the naked sight of each other. Connor crawled back on the bed between Samantha's thighs, his naked body hovering over hers. Samantha throbbed with yearning, hot and eager.

"I want tonight to be just about tonight. I don't want to think about our past, our work, or tomorrow. Tonight, I just need to be with you," Connor whispered against her lips. She felt his need between her aching thighs. He felt her nodding, silently acknowledging she needed him too.

He made love to her all night, overdosing on pleasure, until they fell asleep in joyful exhaustion. It was the first sound sleep for both in a long time.

CHAPTER SEVENTEEN

The Japan Trip

Connor was the first to wake up in the morning, but he didn't move an inch. He wanted to know what Samantha would do when she woke up, if she would freak out and run again. They were spooning, her head resting on his bicep, his other arm wrapped around her waist with his fingers intertwined with hers between her breasts, their legs tangled together under the sheets. He enjoyed the feeling of being pressed up against Samantha's naked body for an hour before she finally started to stir. It started with a soft moan and an easy stretch. Connor kept as still as he could, reminding himself to keep his body completely relaxed, fighting the urge to hold her tightly in place against his body. Samantha rolled over and was staring at Connor's closed eyes. He felt her hand side up his chest. Fingers danced along his jaw before her soft lips pressed against his. He couldn't control the smile that forced itself onto his lips in response.

"I knew you were awake," Samantha's words were nearly a whisper.

"I am now," Connor tried to make his voice sound groggy as he took an exaggerated stretch.

"Liar. You've been awake for nearly an hour, you've just been faking." He was caught but not ready to admit it.

"And what makes you say that?"

"I could feel your heart racing," Samantha said with a knowing smirk. Connor couldn't help but chuckle as he leaned forward and kissed the tip of her nose.

So how long have you been awake and faking then?" he replied.

"For about ten minutes before you."

"And why didn't you get up?"

"I was cozy. Plus, I was enjoying our Mexican standoff." Connor laughed before wrapping her back up in his arms and rolling on top of her, peppering her neck and chest with kisses. "Now I'm hungry." Samantha pushed him off and strutted over to her dresser completely naked. Connor enjoyed the view, trying not to let himself think about what came next.

"What's for breakfast?" He asked from bed, watching her dig through her dresser and slide on a pair of plain cotton panties. Connor couldn't take his eyes off her. She was breathtakingly beautiful.

"That depends, what can you cook?" She levied a flirtatious look at him from across the room, hands on her hips.

"You have a waffle maker?" Samantha's eyes lit up at the mention of waffles. She hurried him out of bed and into the kitchen, barely giving him the time to throw on boxers. Wearing just panties and Connor's t-shirt, she pulled out her never-been-used waffle maker as he started to mix the ingredients. She turned on some music and Connor happily watched her dance around the kitchen, reveling in the feeling that he was finally getting to really see her. She was goofy, uncoordinated, and sexy as hell.

They stood next to each other in Samantha's kitchen eating waffles and not talking. In between bites, they would steal glances at each other, each avoiding asking the question that was burning in both of their minds. What now? After finishing her last mouthful of waffle, Samantha jumped onto the counter and pulled Connor to her, wrapping her legs around his waist to lock him in place.

"I want today to just be about today." Her words came out as a plea. A kiss was Connor's only response before picking her up and taking her back to bed. They spent the rest of the day in bed, touching, laughing, talking, and making love. For a brief time, it felt like they were the same teenagers who fell in love a lifetime ago. They shut out any thoughts of their future. They just lived in the moment, treasuring every second together.

It was early Sunday morning, but they were both awake. They were spooning again, wrapped in each other's arms, trying to pretend there wasn't a world outside the bedroom door they would eventually have to return to.

"I missed you." Samantha was the first to break the silence.

"Missed me?"

"Last week. On Thursday, when you didn't come

into the office. Isn't that silly? It was just a day." It was a small confession, but it mattered.

"I missed you too." Connor brought their intertwined fingers to his lips and kissed the back of her hand. He didn't let the silence overtake them again. The world wasn't waiting and they needed to face it. "I have to go home and pack."

"Okay," Samantha acknowledged his statement but didn't release her hold on his hand or pull away. "I'm going to sleep in a bit more before I start packing."

Connor gently pulled away from her and slid out of bed. Samantha didn't sit up, didn't look at him, didn't move. Connor got dressed quietly and kissed her on the cheek before turning to leave.

"I will see you at the airport in a few hours?" It came out as a question, even though Connor knew he would. Their trip was for work, Samantha wouldn't miss it.

"Yep, I'll see you there." Samantha still didn't look at him. When she heard the door click closed, she let herself wallow in the emptiness for ten minutes before she forced herself to get out of bed and pack. Samantha wandered around her apartment, throwing things in her suitcase absentmindedly. She felt like a zombie, telling herself it was the lack of sleep and stress about traveling internationally for the first time. She refused to admit the truth to herself even when the sight of Connor a few hours later at the airport made her feel alive again.

They boarded and Samantha was comfortable in her first-class seat next to Connor. She spent most of the long flight sleeping, pretending to sleep, or pretending to review reports on her laptop. She didn't talk to Connor, but frequently let her body drift across the imaginary boundary between their seats, her knee touching his, her arm pressed against his, her head rested on his shoulder. He never pulled away.

They shared a taxi to the hotel and made plans to grab dinner in the hotel restaurant to discuss the plan for the week after napping and freshening up. Samantha showered and lied down on her bed, but sleep refused to come. Despite how exhausted she felt, her mind was racing with thoughts of Connor. She unpacked her suitcase and pulled out a sexy dress she was suddenly thankful she absentmindedly packed. She did her make-up, hiding the bags under her eyes as best as she could and curled her hair before texting Connor.

Samantha: Can't sleep. Heading to the bar to grab a drink. Care to join?
Connor: Sure. Be down in a bit.

A smile crept across Samantha's lips as she scurried out the door and down to the bar. She refused to acknowledge the butterflies in her stomach and what they meant. She kept telling herself tonight was just about tonight, avoiding thinking about how she felt about Connor, how he felt about her, and what that meant for their future.

Samantha lit up like a kid on Christmas when she saw Connor walking across the bar to her. He was wearing a crisp white dress shirt with the top two buttons undone and a pair of navy slacks, what was becoming Samantha's favorite outfit. They locked eyes across the room as he stalked right up to her. He wrapped his arm around her waist, his hand resting on the small of her back as he leaned down towards her.

"You look beautiful," he whispered intimately in her ear before placing a soft kiss on her temple. The feeling of his breath on her ear made her close her eyes to focus on it. His words sent a wave of warmth across her body.

"You look quite dashing yourself," she replied, placing a hand on his chest. His hand covered hers, pressing into his heart meaningfully. Connor knew he couldn't say the words, but every move of his body unintentionally confessed his love for her. Samantha could feel it in his touch and see it in his eyes, but if he didn't say the words, she could pretend she didn't know. If he didn't ask her for more, they could live in the now.

"What can I get you?" Samantha asked, pulling her hand away and turning toward the bar. Connor took the hint, removed his hand from the small of her back and leaned on the bar. He was exhausted by the cat and mouse game she insisted on playing, but if the options were play her game or walk away, Connor would play all night. Despite all the frustration and rejection, he wanted to be with her. He couldn't bring himself to let her go.

They had a few drinks before heading to dinner, chatting casually about work throughout their meal. Connor hadn't reached out to touch her since she pulled away at the bar. It had only been a few hours, but Samantha already missed the feeling of his touch. He was keeping his distance and as much as Samantha was thankful for it, she regretted that he was.

They rode the elevator together after their dinner.

They were staying on the same floor, but Samantha's room was further down the hallway which meant they arrived at Connor's door first.

"Thank you for a lovely night." Connor smiled at Samantha, keeping his distance. He wasn't even going to give her a goodnight kiss. Samantha was frustrated by the emotional distance between them now, distance she knew she created. She let out a deep sigh, toeing the carpet with her eyes downcast.

"Connor..." Samantha started without knowing what she wanted to say. She looked up into Connor's eyes and bit down on her lip, her words trailing off.

"Yes, Samantha?" Connor encouraged her softly, refusing to make any moves himself.

"How about I come in for a quick drink?"

"If you come in, you won't be leaving tonight." Connor's response was flat and honest. His voice was both an invitation and a warning.

"I know." Samantha kept her eyes locked on his, letting her acknowledgement sink in and seeing the change in his eyes from exhaustion to excitement.

"Let's crack open that mini-bar then." Connor wrapped his arms around her, pulling her into him before placing a passionate kiss on her lips. Samantha let out a soft sigh as he pulled her into his room.

Connor and Samantha spent almost every minute of every day together for the rest of the week. They would wake up each morning, wrapped in each other's arms. Their days were spent working on the merger. Their evenings were spent in a sweaty naked mess.

Samantha was surprised to find out their first day that Connor spoke Japanese. Judging from his reception at Keiretsu Holdings, he was equally charming in every language. His easy nature translated fluently. Samantha spent most of her working hours watching him, not just because his body was amazing to look at, but because she wanted to be more like him. She was trying to understand the way he was able to talk to people, make them feel special. After watching him for a week she realized his secret was simple. He cared. It didn't matter if he was talking to a CEO or a janitor, he was genuinely interested in them and cared about the person they were. It was a mesmerizing trait. Samantha could watch him for hours.

"How do you do that?" she finally asked him one morning after he spent fifteen minutes chatting with the guy who brought their room service about his twin daughters.

"Do what?" was Connor's confused response.

"Treat everyone like they are the most interesting person in the world."

Because I think everyone is, I guess," he said with a simple shrug. He was completely unaware of how special he was. The urge to tell him she loved him struck Samantha suddenly. She choked back the words. Instead she filled her mouth with a fork-full of pancakes and kept silent for the rest of the morning.

Tomorrow was their last full day in Japan. They were scheduled to leave on the evening flight the following day. Samantha was dreading the flight, the return to reality, to her previous life. Still, she welcomed the distance it was going to naturally give her. She was struggling to keep the walls up around her heart. Each minute she spent with Connor he was breaking them down. She wouldn't be able to hold out much longer.

HER LUCKY CHARM

CHAPTER EIGHTEEN

The Other Shoe Drops

Samantha woke up to her phone ringing on their last full day in Japan. Connor was still asleep, so she silenced it quickly without answering. Glancing at her screen, she had three missed calls from her mom. The do not disturb setting on her phone did its job, blocking the accidental three a.m. phone calls. Her mom wasn't very good with time zone math. Still, after three missed calls Samantha knew she would have to call her mom back before she went to work for the day. She needed to get back to her room to pack up anyway, so she kissed Connor on the cheek, careful not to wake him, got dressed, and headed back to her own room.

She looked around her hotel room. It was the exact same as Connor's room, but somehow it felt foreign. She hadn't spent more than a few hours in it the entire trip. She practically lived out of Connor's room, only coming back to her room to grab another set of clothes now and again. She refused to keep her suitcase in Connor's room. It was important to at least pretend even though they practically lived together for the entire week.

They spent every night together since his niece's dance. Being with Connor was better than Samantha could have imagined. She usually needed time alone, at least a few hours every day to herself to recharge her batteries. For some reason, she didn't need space from Connor. She pushed him away when she felt like either of them was close to saying the three words that would change everything, but she never needed space from him. He felt like the other half of her. He felt like coming home. Samantha tore herself from her thoughts and took a quick shower before she listened to the voicemails from her mom.

The first message was standard mom stuff. How Samantha was doing? How was the trip? Call when you're back. A brief reference to a doctor's appointment. The second call there wasn't any message which was unlike her mom. Samantha wondered if it was a butt dial, but the third call was just a few minutes after that. She must have tried calling Samantha right back, hoping she answered the second time. The third message terrified Samantha, not because of what it said, but because of the sound of her mother's voice. It was frantic, broken, overwhelmed.

"Samantha. Call me as soon as you get this, I don't care what time it is. Please...I need to talk to you." At the sound of that voice Samantha was seventeen years old again, standing in the hospital hearing a doctor say her father was dead. Samantha's fingers flew over the digits as she dialed her mother's number, terror seizing her entire body. As the phone rang, she wished Connor was sitting next to her, holding her hand. She physically shook her head to get rid of the thought. She was being ridiculous. She didn't need him.

"Mom? It's me. What is going on?" Samantha tried to keep her voice calm despite the panic surging in her veins. She didn't want to feed her mom's anxiety.

"Samantha! What am I going to do…" her mother's voice trailed off as sobbing began to take over.

"Mom, take a breath. I need you to tell me what's wrong." Samantha's mind was racing with what could be wrong. It had to be something horrible. They didn't have any close family, so there it wasn't likely to be a death. It could have been one of her mom's friends, but that hardly seemed significant enough for this level of a panic attack on her mother's part.

"I don't know what to do, Samantha," her mother's sobs continued, causing frustration to mingle with the anxiety Samantha felt.

"Tell me what's going on and we'll figure it out together, Mom. We always do. Okay? Take a deep breath and tell me what's wrong." Samantha's voice was detached and a twinge cold. Her emotions were equal and opposite of her mother's. She learned quickly the more panicked her mother became, the more rational she would have to be. It was a defense mechanism. One of them had to be responsible and it always ended up being Samantha. She heard her mother take a deep breath and hold it in. Samantha's body tensed as she waited for response.

"I have cancer." Samantha felt like she had been

hit by a bus. She was in shock. She couldn't respond to her mother's statement. Her mind was racing trying to process the fact. Her mother had cancer. There was a silence on the phone as neither woman spoke, each trying to accept the new reality they were living in.

"You have cancer." It was a statement but came out almost questioning. Samantha was hoping her mother would correct her. Hoping she misheard her. She hadn't.

"Breast cancer. Stage two." Her mother began to sob again at the words, as if saying them out loud, admitting them, made them finally real.

"Okay. I'm coming home." Samantha knew that her mother wasn't going to be able to function without her, at least not for the first few days, maybe weeks. That was how her mother worked. When crisis hit, she shut down, paralyzed. Samantha had to take over, take care of them both, be the parent. Samantha snapped into action, powering up her laptop and looking for the next available flight. There was one leaving in three hours. If she hurried, that was just enough time to pack up, check out, and make it to the airport. She booked it without thinking, still on the phone with her mother trying to sooth her.

"My flight is booked for a few hours from now. I should be home in about 15 hours, so early tomorrow afternoon for you. I want you to have a glass of wine, take a hot bath, and try to get some rest. When I get home, we'll figure this out together, okay?" Her mother didn't respond. "It is going to be okay. I'll be home soon."

"Okay. I love you, Samantha." Her mom's voice was calmer, but still had an edge of defeat.

"I love you too, Mom. I'll see you soon." Samantha hung up the phone and focused on getting home. She grabbed items from around the room and threw them in her suitcase haphazardly while she typed out an e-mail to Mr. Slone. She avoided any specifics, hating to share more about her personal life than she needed to. She hoped that Mr. Slone would know her well enough by now that if she said she needed to go home for a few weeks for a family emergency he would know it was serious and unavoidable. Samantha knew by leaving in the middle of the merger she was sacrificing her chance at partnership, but that couldn't be avoided. Her mother was all she had in the world and she needed her. There wasn't a choice. She had to go home for as long as it was going to take.

Samantha was dressed and packed within minutes. She practically sprinted past Connor's room on her way down to the lobby. She didn't let herself even pause in front of his room, afraid she wouldn't be able to resist the urge to talk to him, have him hold her. She knew if he wasn't awake yet, he would be soon. And he would be wondering where she was. She told herself she didn't have time to tell him what was going on. She needed to get to the airport to catch her plane

She kept herself moving, trying to keep her mind from thinking about anything other than putting one foot in front of the other to get her home. She couldn't think about her mother having cancer. She couldn't think about leaving Connor. She couldn't think about her mother dying. She couldn't think about losing Connor. She couldn't think about losing her partnership. She just needed to keep moving and not breakdown crying.

Focus on what is in front of you.

Check out of the hotel. Get a cab.

Check into the flight.

Get through security.

Arrange a ride to your mother's when you land in California.

You can think about everything else later. Not now.

She kept her mind focused on each small task to avoid feeling the pain tearing through her chest.

Just keep moving.

She was at the gate, waiting to board when she finally let herself think about Connor. She knew she needed to tell him that she was leaving. He would be waiting for her to start their workday. Tears peaked in the corner of her eyes when she thought about him knocking on her hotel room door and finding she was already gone. There was so much she wanted to tell him, so much he deserved to hear from her. All she could manage was type out a vague impersonal e-mail.

From: Samantha.Cane@PMTLaw.com
To: Connor.Grayson@RepublicConsulting.com
Subj: Family Emergency
Connor-
Took an early flight this morning. I have a family emergency. I don't know when I will be back. Informed Mr. Slone. Please give my sincere apologies to Hiro and his team.
I'm sorry.
Sincerely,
Samantha Cane
Associate Attorney
Phillips, Morrissey & Tanner

It was less than five minutes later when her phone started ringing. She didn't have to look to know it was Connor. She couldn't talk to him. Hearing his voice, the concern, the disappointment, the anger would break her. She sent his call to voicemail. She did it again the next two times he called immediately after that too. Then the texts started.

Connor: Where are you???
Samantha debated not answering him. Maybe he would think she was already on the plane if she didn't reply.
Connor: What happened?
Connor: Answer me.
Connor: Please.
Connor: Samantha…I'm going crazy here.

She could almost hear the desperation through his texts. Her fingers hovered over the keys, not knowing what to say to him. Not knowing if she should say anything. It was so hard for her not to reach out to him, not to lean on him, not to need him.

Samantha: At the airport. Catching earlier flight. Family emergency. Boarding now, must turn my phone off.

Samantha had another forty-five minutes before her flight was boarding, but she turned her phone off any way.

CHAPTER NINETEEN

The Fight

Connor kept calling and texting her, hoping she would answer him. She didn't. He had no idea what her family emergency was. They went to bed together last night, the same as every night this week, but she was gone when he woke up. He was disappointed to wake up alone, but he didn't panic. He had thought she went back to her room to get another change of clothes. He assumed she would be back and they would have breakfast the same as always. He loved the little routine they had developed. He let himself think they were together, really together. That he meant something to her. She refused to say the words, but he knew she cared about him. Still, he could feel her pull away every time she got scared.

It was just past eight o'clock when Connor started to worry about where Samantha was. His stomach was grumbling, reminding him of the late hour.

Finally, Connor walked over to Samantha's room, knocking gently. There was no answer. He knocked a little louder. Still no answer. Panic began to rise from the pit of his stomach. Connor tried to keep himself calm, telling himself that she must have gone down to the restaurant without him. They had a routine, but they'd never actually agreed to have breakfast every morning. It wasn't a big deal for her to go get her own food.

Connor was standing in the hotel restaurant, frantically looking around for a glimpse of Samantha. She wasn't there. When he pulled out his phone to call her, he saw her e-mail. A family emergency? She was leaving! She hadn't said a word to him and she was already gone. Connor fell back against the wall as the feeling of abandonment washed over him in painful waves. She walked away from him again. Without a word to him this time.

Connor dialed her number without thinking. She didn't answer. Was she already on the plane? He called her again. Voicemail again. Connor was losing his mind. He needed to know if she was running to something or just away from him. If her phone was still on, she wasn't answering his calls. He tried texting, desperately staring at his phone, willing her to answer.

Samantha: At the airport. Catching earlier flight. Family emergency. Boarding now, have to turn my phone off.

That was all the response she thought he warranted. He kept texting, imploring her to tell him what was really going on. She didn't respond. Connor was officially late to his morning meeting at Keiretsu Holdings. He tried to put thoughts of Samantha out of his head as he dialed Hiro's office number and hailed a taxi. She may have run away, but he still had a job to do.

When he got to the office, Connor made his apologies to Hiro and his team for Samantha's absence. He was frustrated when they asked questions about her "family emergency", offering their hopes it was nothing serious. Connor had no idea how to reply. He had no idea if it was serious. He had no idea if there even was an emergency. He struggled to focus throughout the day. Luckily, they had already done most of the work for the week. He finally stopped texting her every hour, realizing she must be on the plane by now. Even if she wasn't, her lack of response was enough to get the message. Whatever she was going through, she didn't want to talk to him.

Hiro offered to take Connor out to dinner for his last night in Japan. Connor usually would have accepted just on principle. Social dinners were a key part of building relationships. But he couldn't bring himself to go out. He was exhausted from an entire day of fake enthusiasm. Instead, he went back to his room that now seemed large and empty without Samantha. Before heading to bed, Connor sent Slone and Rebecca an e-mail summarizing his trip. He gave Samantha a substantial amount of praise. Despite how he felt about her, he couldn't deny that she was more than brilliant during this trip. In addition to her normal business expertise, it seemed like she was trying to be more personable. Connor thought she was opening up. He closed his e-mail with a note that he was going to be taking a few days off. He said he wanted to recover from jet lag and attend to some personal issues before returning to work. It wasn't entirely a lie. He just didn't mention the personal business was Samantha Cane. In the morning, Connor sent one more text to Samantha.

Connor: Changed my flight. I'm coming to see you.
Samantha: Please don't.

It was the first time Samantha responded to Connor since she left Japan. It didn't matter. He was already in the air on his way to her. Even if he had seen her text, it wouldn't have stopped him. He let her walk away once before. He wasn't going to let her get away again. Not without an explanation. He deserved to know what was going on.

Connor showed up on the doorstep of Samantha's childhood home about twelve hours later. Despite expecting him after his text, the sight of him standing on her front porch still shocked her. For a split second she debated closing the door in his face and pretending he wasn't there. Her hands were full enough with her mom. She didn't have the energy to deal with Connor Grayson right now.

"What are you doing here?" The words came out sharp and accusatory. Samantha wasn't hiding how annoyed she was that he came.

"What do you mean what am I doing here?" Connor was just as annoyed that she deserted him in Japan and then refused to answer any of his calls or texts. He saw her last one, asking him not to come after he landed at the airport. It almost made him turn around and go home. Then he reminded himself that she at least owed him an explanation. He wasn't going to leave until he got one. "You disappeared on me, didn't answer my phone calls, and are ignoring my texts. What do you think I'm doing here!" Connor was trying to control the anger creeping into his voice.

"I have been a little busy! I told you, I have a family emergency..." She trailed off, avoiding giving any more detail.

The repetition of the same vague excuse was infuriating. Connor pushed past her into the house. He had been in her house countless times, but this was the first time he hadn't been invited and the first time he used the front door. He smirked at the irony before his eyes met hers and his annoyance returned. She was glaring at him. What right did she have to be angry? He was the one who had been abandoned and ignored.

"Yeah, I got the e-mail. Thanks for that." His voice was thick with antagonistic sarcasm. "And what exactly is this family emergency?"

"What exactly makes you think that you can just barge into my house and start demanding answers to personal questions?" She crossed her arms and stood in front of the open front door, silently implying she wanted him to leave.

"Oh, I'm sorry. I thought it might be nice to know what was going on in my girlfriend's life! You know, maybe I could help. Guys have been known to try that from time to time. Be helpful. Instead of just ignored!" He hadn't intended to call her his girlfriend, but that's what she was. He was tired of her ignoring it, avoiding him, pretending they weren't together.

"I am not your girlfriend!" she shot back.

"Could have fooled me Samantha. We've been practically living together for the past week. What exactly do you call that? Think it goes a little beyond work colleagues." Samantha didn't answer him. She slammed the front door and stormed off into the kitchen where she had been making lunch before he had arrived.

"Great, walk away. That's what you're best at isn't it." Connor followed her, not allowing her to escape.

"Would you keep your voice down?" Samantha snapped at him. Her voice had a twinge of concern in it as she looked back toward the back of the house. Connor vaguely remembered that was the direction of her parents' room. He stood in the kitchen staring at her, trying to take deep breaths to calm himself down. He hadn't come all this way just to scream at her. Samantha ignored him while she continued to chop up vegetables on the counter and toss them into a pot on the stove. He didn't move. She didn't speak. There were in a standoff, waiting to see who would break first.

"What do you want from me, Connor?" she asked exasperated, setting down the knife and looking over at him. He could see she was on the verge of crying.

"I just want to know what's going on." His words were a plea. Samantha's eyes went back to her mother's room before she let out a sigh.

"My mother...has cancer." Connor instantly started to walk to her, wanting desperately to hold her in his arms. She stopped him in his tracks with a single look.

"Don't." Her words of rejection cut through him. She instantly went from vulnerable to hardened.

"Why?" Connor didn't understand. Why was she still pushing him away? He could help.

"I can't do this with you. Not now."

"Do what? I just want to be here for you." His

voice was so gentle and sincere it broke Samantha's heart.

"I'm not some toy that you need to fix. I'm not a damsel that needs to be rescued, remember?!"

"I don't want to fix you or rescue you! I just want to love you."

"I don't want you to love me! You are just making everything harder! I don't need you Connor!" She was screaming at him and she wasn't sure why. She just needed him to go. She felt the tears welling up in her eyes. She wasn't going to be able to stop them. She turned away to hide her face. The fact that she wouldn't even look at him as she dismissed him drove Connor insane. He was on the brink of rage.

"Of course not! The unstoppable Samantha Cane. You don't need anyone, do you? You can do everything on your own." His words were angry and mocking. Connor was trying to hurt her. Hurt her the way she hurt him.

"That's right!" Samantha wouldn't back down. She needed to push him away for good. She needed to make sure he would never come back. She refused to turn around. She refused to meet the anger in his eyes. She had been expecting it for eleven years. It was almost a relief to finally have him tell her off. She knew she deserved it. Even still, his words cut her to the bone.

"Jesus, you're serious aren't you! What the hell is so wrong with needing someone Samantha? Enlighten me."

"It makes you weak." Disgust dripped from her voice. She was disgusted with herself, with her own weakness. She couldn't keep herself from loving him. Connor didn't understand. He felt the full force of her words in his heart.

"So, you think I'm weak for loving you?"

"Yes."

"You are unbelievable!"

"Would you please just leave!"

"Not until you tell me how you do it. How do you keep pushing people away? What is your secret? I want to live an empty lonely existence too!"

"It's easy! You just remember that one day they will leave!" She finally turned around to face him, slamming her fists down on the kitchen counter with a heavy clash. There were standing ten feet apart, but the force of her gaze still managed to knock him back. Her eyes were filled with anger, but the unshed tears in them made her look completely shattered. The sight of her took his breath away.

"One day you will wake up and they will be gone? Tomorrow, next week, maybe ten years down the road, but eventually I will be on my own again. Only then, I won't know how to survive without you. I will be BROKEN! I won't be able to get out of bed or eat. Every breath is exhausting, every heartbeat is painful. I don't want that. I can't be that. I can't let myself become so dependent on someone else that losing them would break me." Her words were frenzied and desperate. Connor stood in the kitchen completely dumbfounded, unable to respond. The force of her confession stunned him. She would never be able to love him. She was too scared of losing him.

"Samantha, what is going on?" The sound of her mother's concerned voice broke the sudden silence of the kitchen. Their yelling had woken her up.

"I'm sorry, Mom. I didn't mean to wake you…"

Samantha was shaking the anger out of her body, trying to regain her composure.

"It's my fault Mrs. Cane." Connor tore his eyes from Samantha's face and walked up to her mother. "I am Connor Grayson. I am a work colleague of Samantha's." Connor held out his hand. Samantha's mother took it, turning to her daughter inquisitively. She was trying to figure out how she was supposed to react to the charming stranger standing in her kitchen who had been screaming at her daughter just moments ago. Samantha was unable to do anything but stare at Connor.

"I am sorry, I'm afraid got a bit carried away. We were working on a big project together before Samantha left. But I was out of line. I was just leaving." Connor's voice was smooth and calm. To anyone other than Samantha, he would have appeared his normal charming self. Only Samantha was able to hear the pain under the forced cheerfulness in his voice. With an apologetic smile Connor was gone. He finally had the answers he waited for eleven years for.

CHAPTER TWENTY

Tables Turning

"What on earth was that about?" Samantha's mother asked as soon as they heard the front door close behind Connor.

"It was nothing. Just a work thing," Samantha lied.

"That was not about work, sweetie. No one gets that upset about work."

Samantha turned her attention back to the pot that was now boiling over on the stove. She completely forgot the soup she was making while arguing with Connor. She began fussing over it, trying to keep busy to ignore the ache in her chest. She needed her mother to stop asking about it. She needed to forget about it. About him.

"Like Connor said we were working on a big project, a merger. He was upset I left before it was finished."

"A merger? Interesting," her mother teased. "He

certainly is gorgeous."

"I'm making vegetable soup for lunch." Samantha ignored her mother's comments, focusing on her soup like it held all life's secrets. Her mother walked up beside her, stilling the hand Samantha was using to stir.

"Samantha, come sit with me for a minute."

"I'm cooking..."

"I heard what you said."

"What I said?" Samantha was playing dumb. She never talked to her mom about her breakdown. The fact that she mentioned it to Connor seemed like a betrayal of her trust.

"About being broken." Samantha's guilty eyes met her mother's. She hadn't meant for her mother to hear her words. She hadn't even meant to say them to Connor. They just flew out of her mouth. For that moment her lips were connected directly to her heart, bypassing any of the filters in her head. Samantha turned off the burner and sat next to her mother on the kitchen bar stools.

"I know you loved your dad and I know it broke your heart to lose him, especially so suddenly." Samantha was surprised at how placid her mother's voice was. They never talked about her father. Samantha was always too nervous to bring him up, afraid her mom would shut down again.

"As hard as it was for you, it was worse for me. I was destroyed. He was my husband, my everything," her voice began to crack slightly at the memory of the love of her life.

"I know. I'm sorry—" Samantha's mother waved off the apology.

"I'm the one who should be apologizing. You had

to be the strong one. I am your mother and I should have been there for you. But I wasn't, was I?"

"It was a long time ago." The truth in her mother's words was a balm on a wound Samantha thought had long since healed. Still, she didn't want to dwell on the timeworn pain. "We have bigger issues to deal with. We need to focus on beating cancer!"

"You are so much like your father. Always with your eyes forward. Determined. Incapable of giving up. When I lost him, it was easier to lean on you than to learn to stand on my own two feet." Her eyes became misty as her hands came up to caress Samantha's face. "You had to hold up the both of us. You still are." The honesty caused them both to hesitate, as if they were venturing into unsteady ground. "I called you in a panic and you dropped everything. You flew halfway around the world to take care of me."

"That is what family if for," Samantha replied easily, giving her mother's hand a squeeze against her cheek. There were times she resented having to be the adult, but she loved her mother more than anything. She would always be there for her.

"Maybe. Or maybe you've been too busy taking care of me to take care of yourself."

"I am fine. I have a great life! I have you, a job I love, and a beautiful apartment." Samantha's words sounded hollow. Her existence suddenly felt barren.

"And when I'm gone? Who is going to be your family?" Her mother's question terrified Samantha.

"Don't talk like that. We'll beat this!" Samantha hugged her mother tightly.

"I hope I do. I hope I live to be a hundred! But, sweetie eventually I am going to be gone. And I don't want you to be alone." Without speaking a word, Samantha buried her face in her mother's shoulder, taking deep breaths, and trying not to panic at the thought of being completely alone.

"You know what the funny thing about love is?" Her mother gently stroked her hair like she used to when Samantha was a little girl. "Sometimes it hurts and sometimes it heals. But you can't have one without the other. You are right. Losing your father broke me." Samantha pulled away from her mother, guilt and tears canvassing her face.

"Mom, I didn't mean—" her mother waved away her words again and continued undaunted.

"Yes, you did. It's alright. I will never be as strong as you are. But you know what?" She paused to meet Samantha's eyes and wipe away the tears. "I wouldn't sacrifice a single second I had with him to make it hurt less." Samantha tried to let her mother's words sink in. She knew they were true. Even eleven years later she felt the loss of her father deep in her soul. She still loved him. It still hurt to think of him, but she wouldn't sacrifice a single moment. She was thankful for every memory. She would go through all the pain again if she could have just one more day with him.

"If you are running away from someone you love, you aren't saving yourself any pain. You're just spreading it out, poisoning your heart a little bit every day, for the rest of your life."

"At least it is manageable!" was Samantha's pragmatic response.

"Is that what you want your life to be, baby? Manageable? Stop worrying about what might be and hold on to what is. Are you in love with him?"

Samantha's mom looked into her eyes and into her heart. She couldn't lie.

"Yes."

"Then, he deserves to know. And you deserve to be happy for as long as you can be." Her mother stood and kissed her on the forehead before walking back to her room.

Samantha struggled the rest of the day trying to argue against her mother's words. She kept trying to convince herself she knew what was best for her life. She tossed and turned the entire night, desperate to hold onto her belief that she was strong enough to live her life without love. Her mind drifted back to their week in Japan. She cherished the time they spent together. She had been truly happy. She threw it away willingly in exchange for this empty feeling. Losing him hurt. It hurt the first time and it hurt now. At two in the morning staring at her bedroom ceiling Samantha Cane had a revelation. She was a complete and utter idiot.

She was in love with Connor Grayson. Losing him was always going to hurt. Sacrificing their love didn't stop the pain. She wanted him. She needed him. She loved him. And now, she needed to finally tell him. She pulled out her phone and thought about what she could possibly say to him.

Samantha: I need you. Please come over.

Samantha didn't know if he was still in town. He might have flown home right after they talked. She laid in bed, curled up with her cell phone, waiting for it to buzz. She was desperate to hear from him. Exhaustion was finally pulling her under when her phone lit up.

Connor: I'm here.

A smile was spread wide across Samantha's lips, her heart raced in her chest. Samantha threw off the covers and ran to the front door, ripping it open only to find nothing there. Her heart dropped. Was he just teasing her to be cruel?

Samantha: Where are you?
Connor: Where do you think?

Samantha ran to the backdoor. She should have realized that was where he would go. He was sitting on the step, shoulders slouched, head down. He turned to face her when he heard the door open. The look on his face broke her heart. It was clear he thought he lost her, yet he was still here. He was here because she asked him to come. He would always come when she said she needed him.

"Is your Mom okay?" he asked gently as he stood up. Samantha threw herself into his arms, unable to control herself.

"I'm so sorry," was all she could say. He wrapped her up and held her close. It was the best feeling in the entire world.

"Sorry for what?" he asked softly in her ear.

"For everything!" She buried her face in his chest, grabbing fists full of his shirt in her hands. She didn't know where to start. She had so much to make up for. "I can't believe you came…"

"Is your Mom…" He didn't finish his question, letting the unknown speak for itself.

"Oh, no! She is fine." Realization dawned on Samantha. He came because he thought something happened to her mother. "I'm sorry. I didn't mean to make you think..." She wasn't willing to say the words out loud either. This was supposed to be about her and Connor. She wouldn't let herself panic at the thought of the fight her mother was facing.

"Jesus, Samantha. I thought..." His voice trailed off as he let out an aggravated sigh. He broke their embrace with a shove. It wasn't violent, but the sudden harshness made Samantha gasp. Connor was dragging his hands through his hair as his gaze drifted up to the sky. She was desperate to see that familiar look of longing in his eyes. All she saw was confusion and exhaustion. He looked like he hadn't slept in days. He looked awful and it was her fault. Silence overtook the space between them.

"I just needed to see you." She had so much to say to him, but after all the years of hiding, she didn't know how. Three little words never seemed so heavy.

"That's it," he snapped at her. In that instant something changed. She could hear the fierce anger in his voice. "I can't do this with you anymore." When his eyes met hers, she didn't see the longing she had hoped for. All she saw was rage and resentment. He turned and started walking away.

"It's not like that..." Samantha was chasing after him, reaching for him while still searching for the words to explain it all.

"Fuck, Samantha! It's always like that. You call me when you want me, get what you need, and then shove me out of your life again." His words were choked with bitterness. She was stunned silent by their truth. Her feet cemented to the ground under her. Her arms now weighed a thousand pounds. She couldn't get to him, couldn't reach out to him. She had been selfish and hurtful.

"But—" she called out to him, unable to move. When he turned to face her the ferocity in his eyes caused her to draw back. He was furious.

"I have been chasing you for eleven years. Eleven years! I have loved you for so long, and for what? To be strung along, teased, and tortured? Trying to be happy with the few moments I can cobble together before you run off?" His words cut like a knife, slicing open Samantha's chest, exposing her bleeding heart. "I deserve better than this. Better than you." He reached in and ripped her heart right out of her chest.

"I—" Samantha couldn't get the words out fast enough. He cut her off.

"I don't care, Samantha. Whatever it is, whatever has you freaked out this time, you'll figure it out on your own. You always do. I'm done." He crushed her heart in his clenched fist before tossing it aside, abandoned in the dirt as he walked away.

Connor, please!" was all Samantha could manage to scream out, still unable to move with the burgeoning ache in her empty chest. He paused for just a second as he got to his car. His resentful eyes burned into her skin. It felt like he was trying to eradicate her with his stare. She felt like she was dying.

"Thanks for everything. Don't contact me again." He slammed the car door and drove off. He didn't look back.

CHAPTER TWENTY-ONE

The Final Chapter

Samantha was devastated. She didn't know what to do. She was completely lost. Broken. She sank to her knees in the yard and pulled out her phone. Before she had time to think about it, she dialed Monica's number and spewed out her entire crazy history with Connor Grayson through pathetic broken sobs.

Holy fuck, Samantha," was Monica's flabbergasted response.

"What do I do? I can't lose him. Not now!" Samantha was desperate. Monica had never heard her like this. Samantha didn't do emotions. She didn't do weakness.

"You seriously are in love with him, aren't you?" Monica was completely astonished.

"I am." Samantha sounded shattered.

"Well, you've fucked up pretty bad. You treated him like shit for a looooong time," Monica drew out the word to make sure Samantha was appreciating the gravity of her fuck up.

"I know that! Damn it, Monica. I didn't call to be told what I already know! What do I do?" Samantha was growing increasingly irritated.

"You aren't going to like it." Monica was dismissive.

"Just tell me! I'll do anything at this point." Samantha wasn't exaggerating. If Connor asked for both of her kidneys, she would hand them over gladly in exchange for a smile from him.

"Grovel. Beg. Plead," Monica's words were flat and honest. "Humble yourself, sweet cheeks. Preferably in public. And even that isn't a guarantee. You've got a lot of ground to make up for."

"I can do that," to her credit, Samantha's voice held zero doubt, but Monica didn't believe she was capable of real contrition.

"Can you? Half-measures aren't going to work here. You need to open yourself up, be completely honest with him, and leave it all on the floor. That isn't exactly your strong suit."

"I have to at least try, right?" Samantha was desperate for confirmation. She felt like she couldn't trust her own trodden heart.

"If he is worth it, yes."

"He is worth it." There was no doubt in Samantha's voice.

Samantha stayed at her mother's for the rest of the week, despite the fact that she was desperate to run back to Connor and her mother continuously tried to convince her she would be fine alone. Samantha was thankful her mother was trying to be strong and independent, but she knew that cancer wasn't something you let someone you loved fight alone. She split her time between developing her mother's treatment plan and plotting how to get Connor back. After several meetings with an oncologist, she was cautiously optimistic about her mother's chances. Thankfully, her detection had been early. The treatment plan was going to be aggressive and grueling, with a mastectomy and radiation, but her chances for survival were incredibly strong. They agreed Samantha would fly back every weekend for the first few weeks of treatment to help. Sunday night Samantha was boarding a plane back home. She was struggling with leaving her mother, but she knew she would be back soon. She had left things with Connor long enough.

On Monday morning Samantha showed up at work in a soft pink dress she bought the day before. It twirled when she spun in circles and was the exact shade of Connor's dress shirt. She was wearing matching soft pink lipstick. Her hair was down in gentle waves. She looked more feminine than she had since she was a little girl. She felt like she was wearing a costume. In a way she was. She was pretending to be the woman Connor deserved. The second she stepped off the elevator she was drawing an alarming number of stares from her colleagues. She took a deep breath, straightened her back, and marched into battle. She went straight to Connor's office. She was hoping that not telling anyone she was returning to work meant he would still be working out of his temporary office at Phillips, Morrissey & Tanner instead of retreating to his office at Republic Consulting. The door was open and she could hear his voice. The hole in her chest ached, but she didn't let her determination falter. She stood in his doorway and knocked tentatively. He looked up from his screen, still talking on the phone. His eyes started at her heels, traced up her exposed calves, took in the full skirt, her narrow hips, her flushed face, and rested on her pleading eyes. His face was unreadable. Did he know what she was trying to say? That this was all for him?

"Could you hold on one second?" Connor put his call on hold and rose from his chair. His eyes stayed locked on Samantha, but he didn't speak a word. Samantha held her breath. Connor slowly crossed the room until he was right in front of her. She could feel his warm breath on her body. He grabbed the door and shut it in her face. She stood there in disbelief as she heard him walk back to his desk and resume his call, his voice never giving away a hint of discomfort. Samantha stormed back to her office, the taste of metal filling her mouth to keep the tears off her cheeks.

"Did you seriously think it was going to be that easy?" Monica's cynical voice held no trace of sympathy through her office phone. "You put on a pink dress and stood in his doorway and he is supposed to forgive you for torturing him half his life?"

"You didn't see the look on his face. It wasn't angry. It was blank. Nothing. It's like he didn't even care." Samantha sounded miserable.

"He cares. Trust me. He wouldn't put up with you this long if he didn't care. But you've got to take it up a notch. You've got to show him how you feel."

"How the hell am I supposed to do that when he won't even talk to me!" she shouted. She was sure

Tammy could hear her, but at this point she didn't care.

"I don't know, tramp. But, if you want to be with him, you've gotta go bigger."

The next time Samantha saw Connor was at the daily merger meeting. Before she would stand in the back of the room and scowl at Connor. Now, she was early to the meeting and found a seat next to where she knew Connor would sit. He arrived late and stood in the back of the room, as far away from Samantha as he could physically get. He was incredibly talented at being evasive. At the end of the meeting, he turned to leave immediately. Samantha tried to make her way through the crowded conference room to get to him. He was already halfway across the office by the time she made it to the conference room door. She called out to him. Half the office turned to face her. She knew he heard her, but he didn't stop. He didn't even slow down. He kept his same quick pace until he was in his office and then he shut the door. The entire office was staring at the caricature that used to be Samantha Cane. Everyone saw him ignore her. She was seconds from storming into his office and making a scene that would go down in office legend until she realized pushing her way into Connor's life wasn't going to win him back.

Connor kept his office door closed for the next two hours, avoiding Samantha completely. It wasn't until the one o'clock conference call with Japan that Samantha saw him again. They were in the conference room, sitting at the head of the table on either side of Mr. Slone with the rest of the merger team sitting around the table. Samantha could feel the anger radiating off him.

"I wanted to discuss the proposal for integrating the billing structures." Samantha recognized Hiro's voice coming through the speakers. "It seems unnecessarily complex."

"In our discussions here, we have considered several possible options, including leaving the current billing structures in place for each region—" Samantha began her explanation only to be cut off by Connor.

"That was ruled out as a non-starter," Connor's voice was stern as he cut her off without bothering to look at her. The entire room shifted awkwardly in their seats at the tension.

"The complexity of each market combined with the fluctuation in the different currencies..." Samantha started again calmly to try to explain her point.

"Complexity isn't the issue. Mergers are always complex. It's about making the commitment and putting in the hard work to push through the issues," Connor stared straight forward, refusing to look at Samantha as his words dismissed her.

"I appreciate the sentiment Connor, but the issues—" Samantha let out an exasperated sigh as Connor cut her off for a third time.

"It's not sentimentality, it's practicality. This can't be one sided. It can't be half-measures. You keep each other at a distance, the merger fails, and both companies are ruined." Connor's words were bitter and indignant.

"Perhaps we should continue our internal discussions and re-attack the issue later," Mr. Slone chimed in trying to diffuse the situation. Samantha and Connor ignored him.

"I'm not saying it's not worth the effort. Some companies are just more open to change than others. These restrictions were put in place years ago because the senior partners were worried about losing the core of the firm's identity." Samantha lost sight of the rest of the people in the conference room, staring intently at Connor, only able to see his profile.

"And you think Keiretsu doesn't have the same concerns? They are making the same sacrifices, taking the same risks!" Connor was livid.

"I'm not saying they aren't. I'm saying they might need to be patient as we make adjustments."

"I think I have shown more than enough patience." His words were thick with meaning. "There are no guarantees. At some point, you just have to believe and jump in with both feet. If you can't do that, then you are just wasting my time with this charade!"

"Charade!" Samantha pushed back from the table, exasperated. "This isn't a charade. I'm trying—"

"Doesn't look like it from where I'm sitting." There was no longer anger in his voice. Connor was dismissive and cold.

"Connor I hardly think that is appropriate. We should all take a min—" Mr. Slone was trying to regain control of the meeting while everyone stared at Connor and Samantha in sheer amazement.

"I can't do this anymore. You win, Connor." Samantha stood up and turned to Mr. Slone. "I need to be removed from the merger team."

"Samantha, this is hardly the place. We can discuss—" Mr. Slone's words were a warning. Samantha was making a scene. She didn't care.

"Mr. Slone, I'm in love with Connor Grayson,"

she blurted out in front of everyone. Half a dozen audible gasps, including Connor's, simultaneously cut through the tension in the room. His entire body shifted in his chair as he finally turned to look at her. Her eyes convinced him of the sincerity of her words. "And I have let it impact my work on this merger. We have a complicated history that I should have disclosed upfront. I think the best thing for the company and the team is for me to step away."

"What are you doing?" Connor was confused. He was still trying to process her words.

"You are more experienced and better equipped to manage the team." Samantha's voice was calm and detached.

"No. Why are you doing this? Here. Now." Connor stood up and leaned in toward her. She was giving up the merger. She was giving up the partnership. She was in love with him. It was all too much for Connor to process. In the span of a few minutes everything he thought he knew about Samantha Cane had suddenly changed.

"Because I should have done it eleven years ago." Her voice didn't falter despite the tears slowly rolling down her cheeks. She didn't try to stop them. She didn't brush them away. She just stared into Connor's eyes, completely oblivious to the rest of the people in the conference room. Connor had only seen Samantha cry twice. The first time was for her father. This time, it was for him.

"You aren't leaving the team." Connor's eyes never left Samantha.

"Yes I am." Even her surrender had to be an argument.

"No. You aren't."

"Connor—"

"Samantha." He cut her off just to make her stop speaking.

"Perhaps this is a good time for a quick break." Hiro's voice rang through the small conference room, temporarily drawing everyone's attention back to the speakers in the middle of the table.

Suddenly snapping back to reality and the scene she had just made, Samantha's cheeks flashed bright red as she left the room at a near sprint back to her office.

"Show is over everyone." Slone's commanding voice sent everyone else out of the room. Everyone except Connor, who was still too stunned to get out of his chair. "Connor, why don't you go and figure out what the hell that was about." It was an order and an accusation. As much as Slone liked Connor, he was at least half responsible for the profoundly unprofessional outburst that just ruined Slone's afternoon.

"Let me know how that goes." Hiro's laugh echoed through the conference room speakers. Connor leapt out of his chair and sprinted after Samantha.

"What happened?" Connor asked, curiosity taking over the other emotions swirling around him as he closed the door to Samantha's office behind him.

"What do you mean?" Samantha wasn't trying to be obtuse. She was honestly confused. Did he not know she had loved him forever? Could he not see she was trying to give him everything he deserved?

"What do I mean? You come here, dressed like the flower girl in a wedding, are suddenly in love with me, and ask to leave the team? What the hell happened?"

He sounded exasperated. This wasn't the happy ending Samantha planned. She was losing her patience. She gave him everything she had to give and still, he was cold and detached.

"You happened! Did you even hear us in there? I can't do this every day. You can finish the merger better without me. And for the record, I am dressed like a flower girl for you. And, I have always loved you!" Samantha was shouting at him without thinking about it. His face was pure shock. He stood staring at her from across her office. There was no turning back now. She had to get the rest of it out. Time to grovel, beg, and plead.

"I fell in love with you when I was seventeen. I loved you so much it scared the hell out of me! I just kept thinking what if I lost you? So, I let you go. Or, chased you away, I guess. Then, I did it again when my mom told me she had cancer. It's not because I don't love you. I do. I always have." Her eyes met his, brimming with a plea to be forgiven. He just stood staring at her in amazement, his face completely blank. Samantha kept going, eleven years' worth of apologizing spilling out of her uncontrollably.

"I don't want to need you. I didn't think I was strong enough. I didn't want to be like my mom after my dad died. So, I just told myself over and over again not to love you. Not to need you. And I thought it would work. Then, last week after we fought in my kitchen, I realized I don't just love you. I love who I am with you. You make me happy. You make me whole. I asked you to come over that night to tell you I love you. But you thought I was just using you. Hearing you tell me you deserve better was excruciating because I know it's true. Don't contact me again. It was unbearable."

"Samantha." His voice was softer. He stared at her, his mouth dropped open in astonishment.

"I deserved every word. I know. It was long overdue." A small honest laugh escaped Samantha's lips. "I am so sorry. For everything. I love you, Connor." Samantha had tears running down her face again. Ever cell in her body was focused on Connor, searching for signs of forgiveness.

Slowly, his face began to show signs of recognition as her words began to settle in his mind. His lips held a hint of a smile. She did love him. As much as he loved her and she always had. The thought sent warm waves of joy throughout his body melting his resentment.

"Talking yourself out of being in love? That is quite simply the stupidest thing I have ever heard." The smirk was wide across his face now. He couldn't help himself. The feeling of the room shifted, tension changed to longing. He was crossing the room to her. Heat built in the shrinking space between them.

"Excuse me?" Samantha said with a mockingly indignant tone. "I'm pouring my heart out here jerk!" She playfully slapped his chest when he was finally standing in front of her. She let her hand rest on his warm chest just above his heart. She felt it racing under her fingertips.

"Say it again." His voice was soft as he wrapped his arms around her waist.

"I am sorry," she whispered against his lips as he drew her to him. He laughed at her apology. The sound spread warmth across Samantha's body even though the laugh was at her expense.

"Those aren't the three words I was talking

about." He leaned down into her, his forehead resting on hers.

"Oh." She melted into him. "Connor Grayson, I love you."

"One more time." He kissed her cheek, tasting the trail of salty tears.

"I love you," she softly moans.

"Again." He trailed his lips across hers and kissed her other cheek.

"I love you," she murmured as his lips gently found their way on top of hers.

"I love you, too," he declared with a kiss. He kissed her as if he had been waiting his entire life to feel her lips on his. Samantha wrapped her arms around his neck and pulled him closer. She kissed him like she was dying and he was the only cure.

"Ms. Cane? I'm so sorry, but Mr. Slone is asking for you," Tammy stuttered, barging in without knocking. Despite the sudden audience, Samantha didn't pull away from Connor. Tammy stared at the two embracing lovers with envy and admiration, like a little girl at the end of Disney movie. Her misty doe eyes left no doubt for Samantha that she had overheard them.

"Tell Mr. Slone I will be with him in a minute." Samantha skipped the standard knocking lecture. "And Tammy, call me Samantha."

On Friday night when Samantha flew home to see her mother, Connor was in the seat next to her. On Saturday morning, she was the first to wake up. She didn't pretend to stay asleep or run away. Instead she rolled over and stared at Connor's sleeping face, trying to memorize every single tiny thing about him, every inch of his skin, his hair, his smell. She was determined to savor every moment she had with him, regardless of what their future held.

"Waffles?" Connor's voice was thick with sleep as he pulled her to him for a kiss.

"God, I love you," was her giddy reply.

Samantha was sitting in Connor's lap, feeding him waffles when her mom wandered into the kitchen.

"Good morning," she announced her presence to the couple.

"Morning, Mom," Samantha squeaked with a blush on her cheeks.

"More work talk?" her mother teased. Samantha got up from Connor's lap and pulled him into the kitchen next to her mother.

"Let me properly introduce you two. Connor, this is Susan Cane, my wonderful and wise mother. Mom, this is Connor Grayson, the man I am going to spend the rest of my life with." Samantha had a smile from ear to ear as she watched the stunned faces of two most important people in her life. Connor was speechless as he stared at Samantha in amazement.

"Well, in that case I am very pleased to meet you Connor. Let me know when you two set the wedding date. I'm going to take my coffee back to my room."

"What was that?" Connor's ability to speak miraculously returned as Susan left the room.

"What? It's the truth," Samantha responded with a smirk, wrapping her arms around his neck and pulling him down for a kiss.

"Is it now?" he teased, pressing soft kisses along her neck. She pulled back from him, her eyes turning suddenly serious.

"I don't want today to just be about today. I want today to be about how I want to spend every day for the rest of my life. With you. I love you, Connor Grayson. I always have. And I'm pretty sure no matter how hard I try not to, I always will."

"Right back at ya, Lucky Charm."

EPILOGUE

Six months later...

"Where are you?" Samantha could hear the stress in Connor's voice.

"Allie and I are at the batting cages with shortcakes," Connor's niece Madison huffed in disgust at her nickname, making Samantha giggle. "We'll be home in a couple minutes."

"Don't rush, I'll just host this party for our entire family by myself. No biggie." Connor was playful but Samantha knew he was getting irritated.

"Okay, Lucky. Keep your pants on. I have to head to my mom's to shower and change, but I'll be over soon. I love you."

"See you soon. Love you too."

Her mother was finally in remission. It was a long and stressful six months. Samantha and Connor flew back almost every weekend, usually together, but sometimes just one could afford to get away until they finished the merger. Connor flew back a few times himself when Samantha couldn't. Over the past six months, not only did Connor become Samantha's family, so did his parents and sisters. Once Connor finally beat down the walls around Samantha's heart, she couldn't keep anyone out. His sisters became her best friends, especially Allison. Samantha loved Allie for all the ways she was like Connor, confident, easy, and loving.

They enjoyed their time back home so much they decided to move back. After spending eleven tortured years apart, Samantha and Connor were eager to make up for lost time. Samantha was offered her dream job, partner at Phillips, Morrissey & Tanner, after the merger but she turned it down. She decided to amend her thirty-year plan, focusing more of the living happily ever after part. Samantha and Connor each put in their notice and were planning on starting their own merger transition company.

Now that her mother was officially cancer free, they were all getting together for a celebration at Connor's house. It wasn't going to be anything too elaborate or fancy, but Connor had been on edge about it all week and Samantha was running out of patience. He was so preoccupied that he wasn't willing to talk about anything regarding their new business. Connor seemed to keep pushing off the decisions. He was dragging his feet on just about everything except preparations for this stupid party.

Connor: ETA???
Samantha: Final touches. Be there in five.

Samantha was dressed in a soft coral dress, putting the finishing touches on her make-up before she drove over with her mom to Connor's house.

"You look amazing." Samantha admired how beautiful her mother looked despite what she had been through.

"Thank you, sweetie. I have a good feeling about today. The start of something new," her mother replied with a brilliant smile on her face. She was practically radiating. Samantha was so proud of how strong she had been, how positive she still was after everything. The quick drive to Connor's house only took a minute, but parking was a nightmare. She kicked herself for not just walking. How many people did Connor invite! She had never seen the street so packed.

The house was overflowing with people, but everyone got quiet as Samantha and her mother walked in. Everyone seemed to turn and look at them. Samantha knew her mother was the guest of honor, but something felt off. She walked into the large living room, smiling awkwardly at everyone until her eyes fell on Monica.

"Oh my gosh! What are you doing here?" She ran to embrace her friend.

"Your better half invited me. I couldn't say no," Monica quipped with a knowing smile. Samantha was happy to see her, but surprised. Connor had gone all out. Pretty much everyone Samantha knew was crammed into this house. Monica pointed behind her, and Samantha's eyes started searching the room for him. She spotted Connor across the room, looking sexy as hell in his white buttoned-down shirt and navy slacks. God, she loved that man. The smile on her face was instant and uncontrollable.

"Samantha..." Connor's voice sounded uncertain,

almost shaky, although he was speaking louder than necessary. It was as if he was trying to make sure everyone could hear him. The room grew quiet as he crossed to Samantha.

"Connor..." Her tone was teasing, although she was growing uncomfortable with all the attention.

"I have a confession to make." He took her hands in his as confusion spread across her face. "This party isn't for your mom. It's for us."

"For us?" Samantha looked over at her mother for an explanation. Her mother looked like the cat that ate the canary, a satisfied smirk on her lips.

"Samantha Cane. I have been in love with you since I was eighteen. God knows you have not made it easy." The room filled with laughter. Samantha wasn't laughing. Her heart was thudding and her mind racing as Connor went down on one knee in front of her. "But I can't imagine my life without my lucky charm. Samantha, will you marry me?"

"Yes!" Samantha screamed, jumping into his arms as he stood up. The room was full of applause, but all Samantha could hear was the sound of Connor's voice in her ear.

"I invited everyone I could think of. There are too many witnesses for you to back out now," Connor hummed as he slipped the ring onto her finger.

"Never," she said with a laugh. "I love you!"

"I love you, too."

They had only been dating for six months, but after half a lifetime of being in love, the engagement didn't seem rushed at all. Being married to Connor just felt right. She knew it wasn't going to be easy. Nothing with Connor ever was. They were going to argue and fight. But it was all worth it. Loving him would always be worth it.

Their first married fight was teasing each other about whose name came first on the company masthead, Grayson & Grayson.

Books by
AMELIA KINGSTON

<u>Standalones</u>
Her Lucky Charm
Truce? Hating Elijah Monroe

<u>So Far, So Good Series</u>
So, That Got Weird.
This is So Happening.

<u>ABCs of Love Short Stories</u>
Adore
Boomerang
Crash

About the Author

Amelia Kingston is a California girl, writer, traveler, and dog mom. She survives on chocolate, coffee, wine, and sarcasm. Not necessarily in that order.

She's been blessed with a patient husband who's embraced her nomad ways and traveled with her to over thirty countries across five continents. She's also been cursed with an impatient—although admittedly adorable—terrier who pouts when her dinner is five minutes late.

She writes about strong, stubborn, flawed women and the men who can't help but love them. Her irreverent books aim to be silly and fun with the occasional storm cloud to remind us to appreciate the sunny days. As a hopeless romantic, her favorite stories are the ones that remind us all that while love is rarely perfect, it's always worth chasing.

Made in the USA
Columbia, SC
14 November 2021

48946104R00133